MOON
RIVER

////

J.R. RAIN

THE VAMPIRE FOR HIRE SERIES

Moon Dance

Vampire Moon

American Vampire

Moon Child

Christmas Moon

Vampire Dawn

Vampire Games

Moon Island

Moon River

Vampire Sun

Moon Dragon

Moon Shadow

Vampire Fire

Midnight Moon

Moon Angel

Vampire Sire

Moon Master

Published by
Crop Circle Books
212 Third Crater, Moon

Printed in the United States of America.

ISBN-13:978-1548509200
ISBN-10: 1548509205

Dedication
To the Source.

Acknowledgments

And a very special thank you to my Street Team! Terri Chapman, Sunshine Hiatt, Joline Novy, Erin Kathleen Finigan, Sheree Beans, Dinah deSouzaGuedes VanHoose, Lynne Lawson, Susan A. Gadbois, Yvonne Roga, D'Aulan Collins, Patricia Boehringer, Evonna Hartshorn, Heather Beyer, Angela Jermusek, Dana Bokelman, Lisa Downing, Jeanie Mueller, Lisa Hollingsworth, Jackie Neubauer, Pat Zunino, Marie Mock, Sherry R. Bagley, Elizabeth Green, Cassie Wilson, Erin Adams, Leah Kilgore, Jodi Brooks, Flora Samuelson, Melissa Grubbs, Tracy M. Golden and Candy Waggener.

1.

*"There is something within me. Something alive. Of
that, I am sure." —Diary of the Undead*

I would miss Judge Judy today, which was
always a damn shame. Judge Judy should be
required viewing for anyone without a backbone.
Tough woman. Fair woman. Scary woman.

My kind of woman.

Instead, I found myself being escorted by a
young cop with perhaps the third- or fourth-cutest
buns I'd ever seen. I ranked his buns right behind
Rand's, the UPS driver who'd turned out to be a
vampire hunter. Officer Cute Buns led me down a
hall that ended up being far too short. I had just
barely started ogling him when he turned to me,
smiled and motioned for me to enter.

I did so, smiling in return, and I think I might
have—just might have—had me some smiling sex.

Whatever that was.

Waiting inside was, of course, Detective
Sherbet. I knew he would be waiting for me because
he'd called and asked me to come down and meet
with him. I also knew he was inside because I could
smell the bag of donuts from the hallway.

Who I wasn't expecting was the tall guy sitting
opposite the detective. He was tall and dark-haired
and sporting shoulders nearly as wide as Kingsley's.
Nearly.

"Detective," I said to Sherbet, who made no
attempt to stand. Rude. Then again, the old detective had been gaining a little bit of weight these
days, and he was veritably poured into that chair.

I heard that, he thought, telepathically catching
my thoughts. The detective, among a small handful
of others in my life, could read my thoughts...and I,
theirs. *I might have put on a little holiday weight.*

*It's the summer, Detective. And there's no
'might have' about it. I'm a trained observer.*

*Well, the Fourth of July is a big deal in the
Sherbet household.*

I grinned. He didn't, although he did look down
at his growing belly.

"I didn't bring you in here to judge me," said
the detective.

"Excuse me?" said the other gentleman, who
had been looking at me, but now snapped his head
around to glance over at Sherbet.

Sherbet, unfortunately, still hadn't quite gotten
the hang of telepathic communication with someone
like me. The old guy would occasionally blurt his

thoughts, rather than think them. *Rookie.*

"Nothing," said Sherbet. He motioned to the partially masticated pink donut with rainbow sprinkles. "Samantha Moon likes to give me a hard time about my donuts."

"I didn't say anything, Detective," I said, shrugging innocently.

"You didn't have to...now, let's cut the crap. Samantha, this is Detective Sanchez from the Los Angeles Police Department."

He stood like a true gentleman, reached over and shook my hand with a firm but soft grip. His grip told me a lot: confident, warm, comfortable with himself. Most important: human.

I'd had my hand in my jeans pocket where I had been holding a hand warmer. Yes, a *hand warmer*. They sold them at the local market...and they did wonders for creatures like me. If I knew a handshake was imminent, I could pop one of these open, grip it in my pocket...and shake hands with confidence.

Sherbet asked me to have a seat, and I did, next to Sanchez.

"Boy," I said. "Two big, bad homicide detectives and just little ol' me. I feel honored."

"Cut the crap, Sam," said Sherbet. "We're going to need you on this one."

Sanchez listened to this exchange and smiled. An easy smile. Friendly. But there was a strength to his jaw, and the way his forearms rippled as he moved slightly. He sported a thick, gold wedding ring. He said, "You were a federal agent, Ms. Moon?"

"Call me Samantha. And yes. For a few years."

"You're too young to retire. Sorry if I'm prying. Call it occupational spillover. Sometimes, I can't stop asking questions."

I nodded. I understood completely. I said, "I developed a...condition."

"A condition that kept you from working as a federal agent?"

"No. A condition that kept me out of the sun. It's called xeroderma pigmentosum and it's a bitch."

"I'm sorry to hear that. And here we dragged you out into the sun. My apologies." Sanchez's concern was real as he leaned forward and looked from me to Sherbet. "I hadn't known. I would have met you at your home, or anywhere that you were more comfortable."

I smiled at his sweetness. "It's okay, Detective. I've learned to adapt."

Truth was, six months ago, I'd adapted quite nicely, as I had then sported a medallion that enabled me to step out into the light of day. That the medallion had been buried under my skin was another story—or that a body-hopping demon had torn it from me...was, in the least, a horror story for another day, too.

Lots of stories, I thought.

Focus, Sam, came the detective's thoughts.

I nodded to him as Sanchez said, "As long as

you're okay."

"Oh, I'm fine, thank you," I said. "So, how can I help you, gentlemen?"

Detective Sherbet looked at me for a long moment. Then he looked at Sanchez, who was looking down at his hands.

"Either someone starts talking about the case, or I'm going to start knocking heads," I said.

That seemed to break the ice. Sanchez chuckled. Sherbet might have grinned. Finally, the handsome LAPD homicide detective said, "We think we have a serial killer on our hands."

There was, of course, no reason why two experienced homicide detectives would be talking to me, a lowly private eye, about a serial killer. Homicide detectives, in general, didn't look favorably upon us. We were seen as a nuisance, amateurish. There was, of course, only one reason why I had been called in. *Something wicked this way comes.*

I had been called in on such a case last year. Sherbet and I eventually caught the bastards behind what had turned out to be a blood ring. Right, a *blood ring.* For vampires. Sherbet, of course, no longer had any memory of my involvement in the case, thanks to Detective Hanner, a fellow creature of the night who had been overseeing—and concealing—the bloody enterprise for many years. Thanks to her otherworldly ability to remove and replace memories, most of the department—and anyone involved in the case, for that matter—

believed that only one man had been behind the killings. The fact that the bodies had been drained of all blood had never made it into police reports or autopsy reports. Any connections to vampires had been removed from documentation. Sherbet himself was remembering more and more of the case, thanks to my help. But much was forgotten and would, undoubtedly, remain forgotten.

Now, I looked at Sherbet and thought: *How much did you tell him about me?*

Sherbet held my gaze then finally looked away. *Everything, Sam. Everything.*

2.

"Sam, he agreed to have his memory removed. About you, about vampires. Everything."

Sanchez nodded, although he kept staring at me. "Whatever it takes to catch the bastard killing these people. That is, of course, if you really are a, you know..."

"A vampire," I said.

"Yeah, that." And now, Sanchez looked a little uncomfortable.

He should look uncomfortable. Either he was surrounded by a lot of craziness, or he was sitting next to something that, had I lost my grip on it, would like nothing more than to drink from his writhing body.

Jesus, Sam, came Sherbet's thoughts. *Dial it down a little. You're scaring even me.*

I'm pissed, Detective.

Don't be pissed, Sam. Sanchez is a friend of mine. A good detective. No, a great detective. He's dealing with something he doesn't understand. You can see how willing he is to find the killer. He'll do whatever it takes.

Still, I fumed. My life was difficult enough as it was, without the world knowing *what* I was. I drummed my longish, pointed nails along the wooden arm of the guest chair.

"So, it's true, then," said Sanchez, watching me carefully. God, I hated to be watched carefully.

"Maybe," I said.

"I told him everything, Sam," said Sherbet. "No need to be evasive."

I sighed. "Fine," I said. "I'm a blood-sucking creature of the night. Hide your kids and all that." I raised my clawed fingers half-heartedly like the vampire in the silent movie, *Nosferatu*. "Rawr."

Sanchez laughed lightly, hesitantly, undoubtedly not sure what to make of all of this. He never took his eyes off me. Hell, if I were him, I wouldn't take my eyes off me, either. It wasn't often that someone met a freak like me.

"You're not a freak," said Sherbet, picking up my thoughts like a freak himself.

"Like hell I'm not," I said.

"Am I missing something here?" asked Sanchez.

"Sorry," said Sherbet. "Sam and I can sort of, ah..."

"Sort of what?"

"Read each other's minds," said Sherbet, and he suddenly looked like he wished he was having any other conversation but this one.

"You're kidding."

"Trust me. I wish I was."

Sanchez thought about that—or tried to—then looked back at me. "I've never met a vampire before."

"That you know of."

"Do they all look like you?"

"Short, cute, spunky?"

Sanchez grinned. "Something like that."

"We look like you, Detective, until you look a little deeper."

"Your skin is pale," he said. "Your nails... they're pointed."

"Very good, Detective. Anything else?"

"Your eyes. They are...never mind."

"They're what?" I needed to know this. I'd seen vampire eyes—Hanner's eyes. And they were wild and not very human.

"You don't blink very much," said Sanchez, but I knew he was holding back. He wanted to say more.

"My eyes look cold," I said. "Don't they?"

He held my gaze, studying me, looking deeply into me. "Yes."

"Like a killer's eyes?"

"Yes," he said.

"Like I'm not all there?"

"Yes," he said again. He held my gaze. He

didn't shy away.

I sighed. When had the change in my eyes happened? I didn't know. Maybe it had happened the instant I had turned. Then again, I wouldn't know since I hadn't seen my eyes in more than seven years.

They don't look that creepy, Sam, thought Sherbet.

Thanks, Detective. But maybe you're just used to them.

Or maybe we're all nuts.

Have they changed to you, Detective? I mean, recently?

I haven't noticed—

Detective...

He sighed, look at me again, looked deep into my eyes, and thought, *Yes, Sam. They've changed recently. Darker, perhaps.*

Evil?

I wouldn't go that far.

"You guys are doing it again, aren't you?" asked Sanchez. "That whole teleport thing."

"Telepathy," I said, winking. "Get it straight."

He gave me a crooked smile. A handsome smile.

A married *smile,* added Sherbet. *His wife is a bit nuts. She would take you on, vampire or not. And she just might win.*

I almost grinned. Yes, someone wanted the world to know that Detective Sanchez was married. I was guessing the psycho wife. After all, he sported a thick, gold band that could have been seen from the Russian Space Station.

Sanchez said, "So, you're really a vampire?"

"That's what it says on the tombstone over my grave."

"You're joking."

"Let's hope."

Sanchez might have smiled. Mostly, he kept his considerable stare on me. I was noticing more and more how he was making the small office even smaller. Either that, or Sherbet was bigger than I thought.

Hey, Sherbet thought.

I grinned, and said to Sanchez, "Tell me about your case."

He said, "Better I show you."

3.

We were driving.

While we drove, I looked through Detective Sanchez's police file. In particular, I studied photos of the bodies. Two women. Both with grisly wounds to their necks. Not so much bitten as *torn*.

"Who found the bodies?" I asked.

"Hikers."

"The same hikers?"

"No. Two different hikers. Two different days. But the bodies were left on the same trail."

"Or killed on the same trail."

"That, too," said Sanchez.

We were winding our way through heavy traffic along the I-5. It was past seven p.m. and the sun had set and I was feeling damn good.

Sanchez glanced at me. "You look a little different."

I was intrigued. "Different how?"

He studied me for a heartbeat longer, then looked forward again like a good boy—or a good cop—keeping his eyes on the road. "I dunno. You have more color in your face. You seem..."

"Peppier?"

"Cops don't say words like *peppier*."

"Sure they don't."

We drove some more. I continued studying the photos of the two dead women. I searched for a psychic hit but found none. What kind of a psychic hit, I didn't know. Hell, I would have taken anything: a face, a name, a distorted image. However, nothing came to me.

"You know a friend of mine," said Sanchez, as he pulled off onto Los Feliz Boulevard—along with about half of Southern California.

"Oh?"

"Well, he's not so much a friend but a great admirer of mine."

I groaned. "Knighthorse."

"How did you know?"

"Because you two are the cockiest sons-of-bitches I've ever met."

Sanchez chuckled. "Does he know about your...secret?"

"No," I said. "Which raises a concer..."

Sanchez, perhaps even catching a whiff of my own thoughts, nodded. "I know what you're going to say: what's to stop me from telling Knighthorse—or anyone else for that matter—your secret? That is, before you erase my memory."

"Right," I said. "For all I know, you could have texted your wife that you're on a ride-along with a vampire."

He chuckled. "Ride-along. Funny. But, no, I haven't texted anyone. Is *texted* even a word?"

"My kids use it, so that's good enough for me."

Sanchez grinned, but then turned somber. "Truth is, I'm damn nervous about having my memory erased. I mean...how much of it will you erase?"

"I can be fairly exact," I said.

In fact, I had been practicing the technique for the past few months with Allison, or, as I called her, my guinea pig. She didn't mind being called my guinea pig, and she also didn't mind helping me practice my various vampiric talents. Mostly, she didn't mind me feeding on her. In fact, she encouraged it.

Strange girl, yes, but there was a reason for her madness—the more I fed on her, the more her psychic skills developed. The more they developed, the stronger she got. The stronger she got, the more of a pill she became.

Sanchez shot me a look. "How does it work?"

"I'm not entirely sure, but I think it's based on autosuggestion."

"Like hypnotic suggestion?"

"Right."

"Are you kind of new to all of this?" he asked. "Being a vampire?"

"Yes."

"New enough. Turns out, there's more to it than running around graveyards at night."

"Do vampires do that?"

"I don't know," I said. "But that's what I always thought. In my 'before' life."

Sanchez laughed a little and made a right into Griffith Park, thus bypassing what looked like hours of traffic ahead on Los Feliz Boulevard.

"I read somewhere that Los Feliz Boulevard is the busiest street in Los Angeles," he said, seemingly out-of-the-blue.

But it wasn't out-of-the-blue. Little did Detective Handsome realize that he was already picking up on my thoughts. I must have been feeling pretty comfortable with him. Comfortable enough that our connection was growing stronger. Granted, getting comfortable—or cozy—with Sanchez wasn't an entirely an unpleasant thought. His psycho wife, however, *was* an unpleasant thought.

As he pulled into a parking space along the perimeter of the quiet park, he looked at me curiously. "Did you just call my wife a psycho?"

"No, I *thought* it. And I'm sorry."

"No worries. She *is* kind of psycho...wait, you what?"

"I *thought* it," I said. "As in, you just read my mind, Detective."

"No..."

"Oh, yes."

"I *heard* you."

15

"You heard my thoughts, Detective. In your head."

"This isn't happening."

"I've said that a thousand times, Detective, but yet, it still happens. And it's happening now. To both of us."

"Shit."

"You can say that again."

"I'm a detective. I don't read minds. I read..." he stumbled for words. The handsome cop looked truly perplexed. He reached up and removed his glasses, rubbed his eyes, pinched the bridge of his nose. "I read police reports, study crime scenes, deal with real facts, real people."

I reached over and pinched his shoulder. "That's for insinuating I'm not a real person." And, yes, I wanted to pinch something *else*, but I didn't want Mrs. Psycho Wife showing up on my doorstep.

"She's not that bad," said Sanchez, and then started nodding. "Yes, I'm aware that you didn't actually say anything, that your words just appeared in my thoughts. I...think I can tell the difference now. The words are softer, whispery."

"Like a ghost," I said.

He snapped his head around. "A what?"

"You scared of ghosts, Detective?"

"Who isn't?"

"Well, you're safe. I'm just your garden-variety bloodsucker."

He kept looking at me. Sweat had appeared on his brow. Some of it had collected at his temple and was about to trickle down. And, as I thought these words, he reached up and wiped the sweat away.

"Yes," he said, "I heard that, too. Does this happen with everyone you meet?"

"No. But this is certainly the fastest."

"What does it mean?"

"Maybe we were married in a past life."

"Are you being serious?" he asked.

"I don't know. I don't think so. But it might explain what's happening."

"And what is happening?"

I gave him my biggest grin. "Congratulations. You've just mind-linked with a creature of the night. Your life, I suspect, will never be the same again."

"Until you wipe my memory clean."

"We'll talk about that later," I said.

He nodded and rubbed that spot between his eyes. His oversized ring caught some ambient lamplight and flashed brilliantly. He got control of himself, took in some air.

"Can we talk about something else now?" he asked.

"Like murder?"

He exhaled. "Like murder. After all, this is where the bodies were found. Come on."

4.

We followed a narrow trail.

Dusk was a special time for me. The disquiet of the day was forgotten. That I could ever feel less than I did now was inconceivable. Now, at this hour, at this time of day, I felt like I could conquer anything and anyone. Literally. I was bursting at the seams. I wanted to climb the highest cliff or tree or whatever the hell was out here. The Griffith Observatory was nearby, with its massive dome that was visible for miles all around. It could see into the universe and all its secrets. *Not my secrets,* I thought. Yes, the observatory would work. Give the astronomers something to really look at.

Mostly, I loved that quiet moment just before I leaped, just before I was about to cascade out into the night, just before I was about to turn into something much greater than I am.

I felt the animal within me wanting out. Nothing that I couldn't control, no. More of a polite request. A mild urging. Was the animal me? Maybe, maybe not. Whatever it was, I briefly inhabited it as this body of mine slipped away. To where, I didn't know. And from where the creature came, I didn't know that either.

Another world, I'd heard. Summoned from *elsewhere*.

Sanchez, who had been leading the way along the trail, looked back at me. "I'm hoping like hell that you just made all of that up."

Oops. I probably should have closed off my thoughts. I didn't want to overwhelm the poor guy. Better to break him in slowly. This was, I suspected, only the beginning of the freaky crap he was about to face.

Then again, maybe a part of me wanted the detective to see a little more, to know a little more about me. Why, I didn't know. I felt a connection to the man. A professional connection, yes. Maybe even a brotherly connection. Or, maybe I wanted him to know what he was in for. What he had signed up for, so to speak.

Or maybe I had a crush on the man and had simply forgotten to shield my thoughts.

Maybe.

So, I did so now, shielding them with an imaginary wall that wasn't so imaginary. It really worked.

"Yes," I said, as I kept pace behind him. "Just a

flight of fancy."

"It didn't seem fancy. It seemed real. I saw it. Or I saw you become something...huge."

"Well, we all dream of being something a little more than we are, right?"

"That was a lot more. That was actually quite fucking cool."

Soon, we were following a narrow trail that wound up into the park. Although the trail was dimming rapidly as the sky darkened, Detective Sanchez picked his way over the trail like a true expert. Myself, I wasn't much of an expert. Although I had spent the early part of the summer hiking through trails on a remote and private island up in Washington State, I hadn't sniffed a trail since then. And, if it hadn't been for my enhanced reflexes and my own version of night vision, I was fairly certain I would have hit the dirt a few times. After all, if there was a tree root, I seemed to find it. Who knew vampires could be so clumsy?

We continued along, picking our way quickly, brushing past only slightly overgrown bushes and plants. For the most part, the trail was well-maintained. Beyond, through the trees, I could hear the steady hum of L.A. traffic. It was an angry hum.

Finally, after about twenty minutes of this, as the dusk was beginning to turn into night, Detective Sanchez fished a small flashlight from his pocket and clicked it on. He shined the beam just off the trail, to a flattened clearing that I suspected had been trampled to death by police activity.

And sitting next to the clearing, shimmering in and out of existence, was a ghost.

A young woman who was watching us.

5.

To my eyes, ghosts appeared as concentrated light energy.

How and why I could now see into the spirit world was still a mystery to me; although, truth be known, it's probably one of the least mysterious things in my new life.

Well, *relatively* new life.

I'd been a vampire now for over seven years, long enough that I almost—almost—forgot what it was like to be mortal. To be normal. To sleep normally, to eat normally, to exist normally.

Then again, what was normal?

Certainly not me, I thought, as I approached the ghost sitting there on the boulder.

She wasn't fully formed. In fact, she was exactly half there. As in, I could see one of her arms, but not really the second. One of her legs hung below her as she sat on the rock...and the other, not so much. The static light particles that composed her ethereal body crackled with bright intensity, which signaled to me that she was a new spirit. Then again, what did I know? I was still fairly new to all of this.

Still, I'd seen my share of ghosts. Hell, I saw them every day. But rarely, if ever, did I talk to them. Most didn't seem capable of communicating. Most, I suspected, didn't even realize they were ghosts. And those that did, had, quite frankly, seemed to have forgotten how to speak. Mostly, I ignored ghosts, because my life was freaky enough as it was.

But I didn't ignore her.

I approached her carefully, nervous that she might disappear into the ether-sphere, as ghosts are wont to do. But she didn't. She jerked her head up as I approached, and that made me wonder...could ghosts actually hear? Surely, they could. Or did she catch my movement? Perhaps they sensed sound waves, or vibrations.

So much I didn't know.

I recalled a little boy ghost who'd come to my front door last year, a lost boy who had been murdered by a sicko who'd lived just down my street. Yes, the boy had definitely heard me and responded to my words.

Ghosts are weird, I thought, as I got closer. *Then again, talk about the pot calling the kettle black.*

"You're all weird," said Sanchez behind me. "And is there really a ghost here?"

"Yes, now shush. Don't scare her way. Stay right there."

I glanced back as he stopped in his tracks, holding up his hands. "Far be it from a homicide investigator to get in the way of a murder investigation."

Shh, I thought to him, and added a mental wink. I liked him. Too bad he was married.

"I heard that."

Oops.

As Sanchez chuckled lightly behind me, I continued along the dirt path, and soon approached the young lady who'd watched me the entire way. She wavered in and out of existence. What prompted a ghost to appear or disappear was beyond me, but I very much wanted to talk to her. I approached carefully, non-threateningly.

I knew there was a difference between ghosts and spirits. Ghosts were still tied to this world. Spirits came and went as they pleased. All looked the same to my eye...except spirits tended to be more fully formed and didn't appear lost or confused or frightened.

This girl was all three.

Also, ghosts tended to take on the look they had at the time of their death...and as I approached the young lady, I could see the gaping wound in the side of her neck.

Vampires, I thought.

Or something mimicking a vampire. Or someone who wanted us to believe it had been a blood-sucker. Vampires, I knew, didn't have to go for the jugular. The jugular was messy. Blood pumped uncontrollably from the jugular. It splashed on clothes and shoes and just made for a helluva cleanup. Much easier to drink from a controlled cut, on the arm or wrist, with no biting involved.

The damage to her neck was too obvious, too vampire-y.

Someone wants us to believe it's a vampire, I thought.

But why? came Sanchez's voice.

You're still in my head?

I guess, he thought back. *Your words just keep appearing, and I keep answering like an idiot.*

You're not an idiot, but I'm going to close you out now. No offense.

Believe me, none taken.

I laughed and put up mental wall, thus sealing Sanchez out. The wall only stayed in place for so long. I'd noted that after a few hours, it tended to fade away, How all of this worked, I didn't know, but I'd learned to work with it, rather than against it. *Swim downstream, not upstream,* as the saying went.

I'd long ago learned how to continuously tune out others. Generally, when I was with Detective Sherbet or my friend, Allison, I mostly pushed aside their own thoughts. Yes, I heard them, but they existed as small background noise that I could tune into, if I chose to. Mostly, I chose not to.

Only with Fang—and sometimes, here and there with Allison—did I pick up long-distance thoughts. Meaning, they didn't have to be nearby. But with Fang's ascension to immortality, well, he was forever cut off from me, just as all immortals were cut off from me.

Hey, I didn't make the rules. I just did my best to live within them.

So, with my mental wall up, and with Sanchez's own internal chattering reduced to low background noise, I approached the dead girl and stood before her.

6.

"Yes, I can see you," I said. "And I know you can see me."

She didn't say anything. I had actually conversed with a ghost only a few times. And only then, I'd simply received *impressions* from them.

This girl wavered in and out of existence. I suspected I might lose her, and so I said quickly, "I want to help you."

I was getting a very strong impression that she was terrified, even in death. Terrified by what had happened to her, and by what was happening now.

"It's going to be okay," I said. "No one can hurt you now...or ever again."

Whether or not she heard me, I didn't know. She continued staring at me, sitting there on the rock, her knees pulled up to her chest, head slightly tilted, revealing the ghastly wound that somehow looked even more awful in death, a wound composed of tens of thousands of glowing light particles. The wound, I saw, was deep. Someone had literally torn open her neck. Yes, she would have bled to death quickly.

"I'm sorry someone hurt you," I said.

She hugged her knees tighter. Her feet were mostly not there. Sometimes they wavered into existence, but mostly, her legs stopped at the ankles. She had been wearing Asics running shoes.

She'd been attacked in the park, while running.

As that thought occurred to me, I caught a psychic hit of her running up a trail. I turned...that trail there, which led off down the hillside and through a tangle of gnarly little trees. Yes, she'd been running up there when something powerful had overwhelmed her...knocking her down, pouncing on her.

And then pain. So much pain.

And that was it.

Her next memory was of sitting beside her dead, broken body.

That had a familiar ring to it. I, too, had been attacked in a different park, while running. Of course, I hadn't been left to die, to bleed out, as I'm sure this girl had. I had been given vampire blood...no doubt by my attacker himself.

Of course, I would never know the truth, since my attacker—a very old and powerful vampire—was now dead at the hands of a vampire hunter named Rand. I'd recently had the pleasure of working with Rand and his merry band of vampire-hunting misfits, in a faraway land in a remote mountaintop castle. Lord help any vampire who crossed paths with those badasses.

Anyway, her plight was familiar to me, even if the end result was far different.

This could have been me, I thought. *Dead and lost and wondering what the hell had happened to me.*

Truth was, had I been killed that night, I probably would have never known what had happened to me. I had been hit hard and ravaged and it all had been a blur...and I had awakened the next morning in a hospital, lucky to be alive.

Lucky to be able to see my kids.

This girl wasn't so lucky.

Then again, I had a certain fallen angel named Ishmael who had, no doubt, something to do with keeping me alive. Which led to another question: how had Ishmael managed to convince the old vampire to attack me—and to keep me alive? To feed me his blood?

I didn't know...but suddenly, I wanted to find out.

But this girl hadn't been part of a fallen angel's nefarious plan to find love, to break his immortal bond with the living by turning a mortal *im*mortal, thus freeing him from servitude.

A twisted, reckless way to go about love.

If it was love.

I suspected it was closer to an obsession. Anyway, luckily, the fallen angel, Ishmael, had mostly kept his distance. For now.

"Do you remember who attacked you?" I asked the girl. "What did they look like?"

She didn't move, but the light filament around her, the thousands and thousands of light filaments, shook and scattered and reformed. She was sobbing.

Her attack had been violent, sudden. I knew this. She might not have seen her attacker. I hadn't seen my attacker.

Or, if I had, I couldn't remember.

But maybe someday I could remember.

And if I could remember the night I was attacked...maybe a lot of what happened to me would make sense.

Maybe.

As she wept, her etheric body shuddering, I saw something else: a bulge at the back of her neck. The bulge was undoubtedly caused by a protruding bone. Of course, in her current state...it was only a *memory* of a protruding bone. Not actual bone.

I went back to the edge of the clearing, where Sanchez was watching me. He had been intently scanning the surrounding area, ever the homicide cop.

"Had her neck been broken?" I asked.

"Did the ghost tell you that?" he asked. "And did I just ask you if a ghost told you something?"

"You did, and, no, you're not losing your mind. At least, not at the moment. We'll see how you hold up when this is all over."

"And what's *this*?"

I thought about that. The night was chilly, but nothing my immortal flesh couldn't handle. The detective, on the other hand, kept both hands in his jeans pockets in an effort to look both cool and keep warm. Guys.

I said, "Someone wanted to make sure this attack was obvious."

"Obvious that it was a vampire attack?"

"You catch on quick," I said.

"So, is there some sort of vampire war that the rest of us mere mortals aren't aware of?"

"You've been watching too much *True Blood*, detective. Vampires live discreetly, kill discreetly. The ones I know enjoy their anonymity and try like hell to exist in the real world."

"So, why would someone want us to think this was a vampire attack?"

"A good question, Detective, but one I don't know the answer to. At least, not yet. And the girl —"

"You mean ghost."

"Yes, the ghost doesn't know anything. She didn't see who attacked her."

Sanchez shivered a little. "Kind of creepy to think that these woods are full of vampires and ghosts."

"And nervous cops with guns."

"Touché ," he said. "And you promise to wipe my memory clean of all of this later?"

"If you want."

"I very much want."

7.

We were at Zov's Bistro.

Yes, the same Zov's Bistro where I often saw one of my favorite thriller writers. I loved his books, but I didn't love his fake hair. He was here now, eating with his wife, and looking very serious while he did so. That was okay. I liked my thriller writers looking serious.

"Do you read his books?" I asked Allison as we were seated.

"Whose books?"

"His books." I pointed at the little man, and told Allison his name.

"Never heard of him."

I stared at her. "Do you even like to read, Allison?"

"I read magazines."

"Books, Allison. Do you read books?"

"Not really. They're kinda, you know, boring—wait, I did just read a book."

As she said the words, I saw the book in my mind's eyes. Yes, Allison and I were deeply connected. Too connected. "You read a book on *witchcraft*?"

"On Wicca," she said, lowering her voice. And this might have been the first time I'd ever heard Allison lower her voice. "There's a difference."

"Enlighten me."

She was about to when the waitress came by and took our drink orders. White wine for me, red for Allison. I would have preferred a margarita, or something fun and foofy. Sadly, my body barely tolerated the white wine.

Zov's Bistro was a quaint, upscale restaurant with reasonable prices in exchange for uncommonly good food. At least, that's what I was told, since I hadn't eaten regular food in seven years. No, I came here for the ambiance...and sometimes a raw steak. Raw steaks didn't always do it for me. The blood that pooled around the steak had been warmed and seasoned and so wasn't pure enough. Anything impure—i.e., not blood—was liable to get a violent reaction from me. And by violent, yes, I mean projectile vomiting.

The local writer, I noted, was staring at me. I remembered back in the days when he was bald. He looked good bald. He looked serious and kind of sexy. Like a literary Burt Reynolds. The fake hair looked disturbing. And it wasn't just a little fake. It was a massive pile of it. Thick and proud and weird. In a way, I admired him for it. After all, if you're gonna get transplants—and not fool anyone in the process—then, by God, you might as well go all in.

"You seem way too fixated on the poor man's hair. I think it looks nice," said Allison, picking up on my thoughts. Generally, I didn't close my thoughts off to Allison. Lately, I'd been thinking of her more and more as a sister.

"I'm glad you think so," said Allison, "because there is a good chance that, in a past life or two, we very well could have been sisters."

"You're losing me."

"It goes back to the book on Wicca...and someone else."

I saw the old lady in Allison's mind. And it wasn't just any old lady...

"Since when do you see ghosts?" I asked.

"Since last week."

She told me about it. Allison had been hired by a man to help him find his daughter's killer. She had done so, and strangeness ensued. "But I'll tell you about him another time," she added.

However, I had already caught her thoughts regarding him. I shook my head at the wonder of it all, and said, "Fine. Tell me about the old lady."

"She's one of us," said Allison.

"What the devil does that mean?"

Allison gave me another image, this time, of the old lady looking not so old. She was younger now, our age, mid-thirties—although I would forever look in my late twenties. At this younger, more youthful age, the woman looked frustratingly familiar.

Allison was nodding. "See, you recognized her, too."

Our drinks came and Allison dove into hers. Literally. Head first. When she pulled away, wine sparkled on her lips. Lips that were smiling contently. The girl liked to drink.

"What's going on, Allison?"

"We're soul mates, Sam. We've always been soul mates, and so is Millicent. There are three of us. Bound together throughout time and space."

"I just met you last year," I said, sipping my wine. I had to sip it. If I drank it too fast, I'd get stomach pains. Who knew vampires would have such sensitive stomachs? Granted, it could be the thing that lived within me who had the sensitive stomach. The thing that I kept alive with each consumption of blood. Knowing that I was simultaneously keeping something wicked and hideous alive, while at the same time keeping myself alive, was something that, to this day, I hadn't quite wrapped my head around.

"Yes, we just met," said Allison, "but we were *supposed* to meet. It was destiny."

"You were the fiancé of a murder victim," I said. "Destiny arranged for your fiancé to die so that we could meet?"

Allison looked down immediately into her wine. The strangeness of her fiancé's murder did nothing to diminish her loss, and I reached out and took her hand and apologized from my heart. "Sorry, that was harsh."

"It's okay, Sam. And I can't begin to understand how the world works, or how the Universe works, or even how God works. For all I know, they're all one and the same. But, somehow, someway, we came together, but this time, as friends."

"And we were sisters before?"

"Often," said Allison, perking up a little. The wine might have had something to do with that. Hers, I noted, was nearly half gone. "And sometimes, brothers. But we'll call that a failed experiment."

I laughed. "I prefer being a girl, thank you very much."

Allison giggled. "Likewise."

"And the old woman—"

"Young woman," Allison corrected. "Millicent."

"Yes, Millicent. She is also a soul mate?"

"Yes."

"But, she is in spirit, passed on?"

Allison shrugged. "She was a soul mate who got here a little earlier this time, perhaps to pave the way for us..."

I caught the thought that she didn't voice. I said, "Or perhaps to guide you in spirit."

"*Us* in spirit, Sam. You are deeply connected to her, too."

"This is weird," I said.

The waitress came by and took our orders. I wasn't in the mood for raw steak. I told the waitress I was just here for the wine. She smiled weakly at that. Allison, of course, ordered enough for two people.

When the waitress left, I said, "Two baked potatoes?"

"They're earth energy," said my friend, who tilted back the rest of her wine.

"You lost me again."

"Earth energy, Sam. They're grown within Mother Earth, and she has infused them with her love and energy."

"Love and energy?"

"Yes."

"Do you know how crazy this sounds?" I asked.

"Says the vampire."

"Fine," I said, taking another sip of wine. "Tell me about the book on Wicca."

"Millie gave it to me."

"The old lady?"

"The young lady. Yes, her."

"And she gave it to you why?" I asked.

"Because, Samantha Moon, you're not the only freaky one in our little duo. I'm a witch, you see."

8.

"A witch?" I said.

"That's right. I said witch."

"Since when?"

"Since forever, Sammie. It looks like I've been one throughout the ages. And since you and I have been sister soul mates, so to speak, I suspect you were one, too. Along with Millie."

"Trust me, I'm no witch."

"Well, not now, silly. You can't be both a witch and a vam—"

"Shh," I said. Allison always had a bad habit of talking louder and louder, especially when the booze was flowing. "Maybe we should keep our voices down, huh?"

"Oops, sorry. I'm just, you know, super excited."

But her excitement was short-lived. A moment

later, she turned her head and buried her hands in her face and I was left staring at her in confusion.

That is, until I saw the image of a thirty-something man in a schoolroom...and then the image of that same young man lying dead from multiple wounds over his face and neck. All of this, I knew, was from the perspective of Allison.

Something very bad had happened to her—and something worse had happened to the man lying dead at her feet. What exactly had happened, I didn't know.

But first things first. I rushed around the table and knelt next to her and hugged her tight and as I did so, she wept silently into my shoulder.

***

A few minutes later, after the waitress had asked if everything was okay and all eyes were on us, I stepped away from Allison and went back to my seat.

I didn't care that all eyes were on us. I cared about my friend and that something very bad had happened to her, and as we looked at each other across the table, as our wine glasses sat forgotten and the water glasses collected condensation, I saw all that she had been dealing with this past week...and, in particular, what had happened just the night before.

When she was done, and I had seen further and deeper into her than I had ever seen before, I reached across the table and took her hands and told her over and over again that it was not her fault.

A man, after all, was dead because of her newfound skills.

Skills that were, to say the least, jaw-droppingly powerful.

"You see, Sam," she said, speaking for the first time in many minutes, "I'm a freak like you, after all."

"Maybe freakier."

She laughed lightly. "I doubt that."

"It wasn't your fault, Allie. He tried to kill you."

She broke our contact and reached for her wine glass, but didn't pick it up.

"And you should have called me," I said.

"I know. I just...I just didn't think things would get so out of hand."

"He was a child killer...and desperate. Anything could have happened. You got lucky." *And,* I added telepathically, *you're not immortal. He could have killed you.*

Allison nodded again and wiped her eyes and finally did lift her glass of wine. When she set it down again, it was quite empty.

We talked more about her newfound skills, about Millie and about Peter Laurie. We talked about his little girl and her art work.

"I promised I would help find good homes for his daughter's artwork."

"I would be honored," I said. "Put me in for two."

Allison laughed, and we shared a quiet moment, holding hands again across the table. The waitress soon brought Allison's dinner, which looked heavenly. It was also, I noted, vegetarian.

"Since when did you become an herbivore?" I asked.

"Since discovering that abstaining from meat helps me tune into Mother Earth."

"Mother Earth?" I said.

"Yes, Wicca is an earth-based religion that draws power from the energy of the Earth itself."

"Of course," I said. "Who doesn't know that?"

"Don't you dare laugh, Samantha Moon, who just so happens to draw her own power from blood —"

"Shhh," I hushed. "You talk too loud."

"I talk the way I talk. You're just going to have to deal with it."

I rolled my eyes. "So, is this the new you?"

"The new and empowered me," said Allison.

"Fine. Then tell the new and empowered you that we have some important secrets that we don't need the world knowing."

"Fine," she said, and happily dug into her salad.

It had, of course, been a long, long time since I'd had anything like a salad. My mouth watered, which was a useless leftover trait from my human days. Still, the salad, with all its bright veggies and leafy greens, looked incredible...and crispy. The crispy part was proven to be true as Allison bit into each forkful. She crunched her food in a way that

41

made me long for cucumbers, tomatoes, and lettuce dressed in a nice balsamic vinaigrette.

I sighed and looked away, and my thoughts turned to my own problems.

"Do you want to talk about it?" asked Allison, between bites. She had also, somehow, managed to order another glass of wine without my knowledge. Maybe she had a telepathic link with the bartender. Wouldn't surprise me.

"Rude," said Allison, picking up my stray thought.

"Sorry," I said. "I'm just cranky."

"I would be, too, if I couldn't eat. So, let's get back to what else is making you cranky."

I nodded. She had, of course, picked up on my brooding thoughts...and what I knew I had to do.

"You're going to break up with him," she said.

By *him*, she was referring to my boyfriend of the past four months. Russell Baker was a professional boxer and about the sexiest thing I'd ever come across. He was also, of course, the man who had killed Allison's fiancé. Or, at least, that's what we had initially figured.

Turned out, the case had been far stranger than originally thought, and Allison never held a grudge against him, and as well, she shouldn't.

"Yes," I said. "I'm breaking up with him."

"Why?"

I thought about it again with a heavy heart...then told her why.

9.

We were jogging Tri-City Park.

The park connected three cities: Fullerton, Brea and Placentia, cities that didn't mean anything to anyone outside of Orange County. Truth was, I wasn't sure which city the park was actually in. I liked to think that with each one-third loop around the park I was entering a new town. I was easily amused.

My jogging partner was Russell Baker. He was a professional boxer and, I guess you could say, my kind-of boyfriend. We'd been dating now for six months, and we seemed to be committed enough, although no one had said much of anything about anything. Meaning, we'd never discussed our situation. We just sort of *flowed*.

I saw Russell about twice a week, which was enough for me. Maybe I wasn't ready for more, I don't know. Or maybe Russell and I didn't have enough chemistry. We were always comfortable, relaxed, friendly...and yes, passionate, too. But the passion didn't extend much further than the bedroom.

The evening was warm. It was early summer. School had just gotten out. I would have my kids for the next three months. A good thing on the one hand: I could sleep in. My kids knew my super-secret identity, and kept it brilliantly, including secrets of their own.

That my kids had to go around keeping so many secrets was something of a burden for me. I hated knowing that I had inconvenienced them. Lord knew I tried to keep it all from them...I just couldn't. Not consistently.

Granted, it hadn't all been bad. Truth be known, our combined freakiness—my immortality, my son's super-strength, and my daughter's ability to read all minds—had brought us closer. It was a sort of *us versus them*, and it was nice.

For now.

We'd see how this all played out.

As we jogged, Russell and I chatted amicably, easily, neither of us out of breath. My shield was up with him, as usual. It was always up. Otherwise, he would probe, unknowingly, deep into my psyche. He would have been surprised as hell by what he found in there.

No, Russell did not know my super-secret identity. I had purchased a lifetime supply of hand warmers, which I kept in my pockets at all times, so that when he and I held hands, there was some semblance of warmth. Granted, there wasn't much warmth when we were body to body, but I didn't think Russell had noticed how cold my flesh might have felt in those intimate moments.

Afterward, I rarely lay naked next to him. I would jump up, pretend to use the bathroom, then get dressed and lay next to him again.

It was weird. He knew it was weird, but never said anything about it.

For us to work, for us to make it to another level, I would have to trust him with my Big Secret. And I would have to trust him without controlling his mind, which I swore to myself that I would never do.

He knew about my inability to go into sunlight, and he knew I wasn't much of an eater. I also suspected that he knew I was keeping something important from him.

Boy, was I.

Hardest of all was that Anthony had fallen in love with Russell. And why wouldn't he? Russell was a professional fighter...and we had gone to his last two big fights. One in Los Angeles, and one in Vegas. Anthony was Russell's biggest fan.

Not to mention, I had spent the last six months shielding my thoughts from him, which got exhausting. Russell and I had developed an almost immediate psychic link, much like I had with Detective Sanchez. Except, with Russell, I could never fully *go there* with him.

I wasn't sure why. I think, perhaps, out of a need to have a *real* relationship. To be as normal as possible. Except, being normal was proving exhausting and almost impossible. I spent half my time lying to the poor guy. Yes, lying came easily to private investigators. We lied to get what we wanted—we pretended to be other people, other occupations, whatever it took to close a case.

I'd found that once the lies had started with Russell, I just couldn't take them back...and I didn't want to be known as a liar. I didn't want him to think he couldn't trust me.

But, nevertheless, I was indeed fibbing to him. I was a fibber. The whole damn relationship was built on fibs.

"You're quiet this evening, Sammie. Are you okay?" Russell asked. His voice was silky smooth. His movements were silky smooth, and they were in the bedroom, too. The man had full control over his body...and what a body it was.

Sadly, he also thought that we were closer in age than we really were.

He thought I was mortal.

I lied about the food I ate.

The drinks I drank.

I lied about my friends.

About my kids.

About the real reason for my divorce.

I lied about everything to him.

Yes, I probably should have come clean about it

all...but once the lies started, I couldn't take them back. And I didn't want him to know what a monster I really was. He adored me. I knew he did. His interest was genuine, real.

He didn't deserve me or my lies.

As we jogged, I turned to him. "No, I'm not okay," I said. "We need to talk."

10.

We stood together on a little bridge.

The bridge spanned a stream that flowed into the bigger pond...or maybe it was the other way around. Maybe the pond flowed into the stream. Hard to say since the water was mostly stagnant and smelled. Beneath the dark surface, I could see glowing torpedo-shaped fish swimming idly. I could see other forms glowing, too. Water spiders and flying insects. Most life gave off a sort of bio-luminescence, at least to my eyes. I could see anything living at night. And sometimes things not living, too.

I see all, I thought.

I was, I suspected, the ultimate hunter.

Anyway, Russell and I were both leaning against the wooden railing. The park was mostly empty at this hour, as it should be. No one but vampires and professional boxers should be out jogging in a city park at night.

There was, however, a man who strolled casually off on the far edge of the lake, hands behind his back, whistling softly to himself. To my eyes, in the dark, he looked very bright, his aura shining a radiant blue. I knew of such special auras, although I rarely saw them. *Blue* meant that he was deeply spiritual, and the brighter the blue, the more spiritual. His was a brilliant sapphire blue that extended far beyond his body. Who he was, I didn't know, but I suspected he was a true master. As such, he had nothing to fear from the dark. Indeed, all good things were attracted to such masters, and they, in turn, radiated good things. I wondered what he would make of me.

I sensed Russell's rising anxiety. He knew that nothing good was going to come from the talk. I could almost hear his heart beating, too. Lord knew it certainly wasn't my own lackadaisical heart, which tended to beat once every ten seconds or so, if that.

I'm so very, very weird.

At the far side of the lake, the bright blue light stopped. Within the blue light, I saw the man turn and face me, his hands still behind his back.

As I stood there on the ridge debating what I needed to do, I sensed a warm tingling come over me. Almost never does the word *warm* ever apply to me, and so I perked up at the rare sensation.

Russell hadn't moved, and there was no wind.

There was, in fact, no obvious source of the warmth, which now surrounded me gently, as if with loving arms. The hair on my neck and arms stood on end, too, but not because I was cold, but because something alive and warm was moving around me.

It's him, I thought, looking again at the figure at the far side of the lake, a figure who was still facing us, hands still behind his back.

I knew that no one but a fellow creature of the night should be able to see us. In fact, I doubted that Russell even knew there was a man watching us.

But he wasn't a creature of the night.

He was, I suspected, just the opposite.

Something holy, something filled with light, something that repelled creatures like me.

But he wasn't repelling me now.

No, he was reaching out to me. It was, in fact, *his* warmth surrounding me.

"So, what did you want to talk about, Sam?" said Russell. He didn't turn his handsome face toward me. He continued looking out over the bridge, out toward the black lake. The lake wasn't so black to me. It was alive and well, and shining with more light than I would ever have dreamed possible.

"Release him, child," I heard a voice say. A voice, I was certain, that had come upon the wind.

For a moment, I thought it had been Russell who had spoken to me...but no, the voice had come from over the lake, drifting to me on warm currents.

Drifting to me from *him*.

Was that you? I thought, looking out toward the man who was still watching us.

I didn't get a response, but I still felt the warm current moving over the water, enveloping me completely. As I reveled in it...after all, it was so rare that I felt warm these days, the full impact of the words hit me: "Release him, child."

Release who? I thought. But I didn't get an answer.

I looked again at Russell, who was now watching me. I could see the concern in his eyes. He knew what was coming.

"Sam," he said. "I know what you're going to say, but please don't say it. Please. I'm happy. We're happy. Don't say the words, okay?"

When I looked back over the water, the figure had continued on, moving slowly. His blue aura shined brighter than ever.

Release him...release Russell?

"Russell, I haven't been entirely honest with you—"

"Samantha, I don't care. I don't care if you're a mass murderer. I can't lose you."

I blinked, processing. "You don't care if I'm a murderer?"

"No, Sam. I need you. I love you."

We had, of course, never talked about love, although I sensed that we had been getting closer.

Release him, child...

As Russell stared down at me, as he took my

hand and held it tightly, I suddenly realized why he didn't care if my hands were cold, or that my body was cold, or why I never ate. Russell didn't care if I was cold, or different...or even a mass murderer.

I suddenly knew what the words meant, words spoken to me on the wind by a blue-aura master.

Russell, I suspected, was bonded to me.

11.

"What, exactly, does *bonded* mean?" asked Allison over the phone.

It was later and I was heading home. Unfortunately, I had been unable to release Russell Baker as the voice had asked. I hadn't intended to *release* him...I had intended to *break up* with him, as normal people do.

But you're not normal, Sam...and you never will be again.

Truth was, I had been too stunned by the revelation that another human being was bonded to me, to think clearly. I had made up some lame excuse of wanting to talk about him and the dangers of fighting...and Russell had said he would give up fighting for me.

Give up fighting.

For me.

My head was still spinning.

Yes, I had intended to break up with Russell Baker, although he'd done nothing wrong—and I had done *everything* wrong. I had lied to him from day one...but, I now knew, he would forgive me for the lies. He would have forgiven me for anything.

I saw the look in his eyes, heard it in his voice. *Bonded.*

"You never noticed it before?" Allison was asking.

"No," I said. "I just thought he was, you know, *into* me. I just thought he was agreeable. Sweet."

"And the more he agreed to, the worst you felt."

"I always felt bad," I said. "I mean, he has no idea who I really am."

"So tell him, Sam."

I opened my mouth and closed it again. The road before me was empty as I drove through the night along the hilly Bastanchury Road, heading home. Yes, I'd considered telling Russell a hundred times about my super-secret identity, and a hundred different times I had talked myself out of it. His life was normal. His life was pure, uncomplicated. Sure, he'd chosen a rough route as a professional fighter. But it was still *normal*. The moment I had opened my mouth about who and what I was, his sweet, simple, uncomplicated life would be thrown upside down.

"Well, your uncomplicated life was thrown upside down," said Allison, following my train of thoughts.

"Yes," I said, "and the one person who could have stepped in to keep it that way, didn't."

"Ishmael," said Allison, referring to my one-time guardian angel who had, in fact, set me up. Yes, Allison knew my entire story inside and out. Hell, she knew me inside and out.

"Yes," I said. "And I hate him for it. And I'll hate him forever."

Even as I spoke those words, something flashed across the sky through my windshield...something that could have been an errant headlight, an advertising spotlight...or something else. A fallen angel, perhaps.

"What the hell was that?" said Allison.

"You saw it?" I asked. Then I remembered her psychic specialty was remote viewing. Undoubtedly, she was right by my side as we were talking, in a metaphysical sense, of course.

"Yeah, and that was weird."

"Welcome to my life."

"*Our* lives, Sam. We're kind of in this together."

I took a deep breath, held it longer than humanly possible, and then came to a stop at a red light near St. Jude Hospital. "I don't want to be the one responsible for introducing him to a world of vampires and werewolves...and witches."

"He's already in it, Sam. He just doesn't know it yet."

"Maybe it's better to keep it that way. Ignorance is bliss, and all that."

I continued through the green light, and then made a left turn into a housing tract.

"I can't tell you, Sam, if it's right or wrong to tell him. But I think he has a right to know who you are and the real reason you are breaking up with him."

"Maybe," I said.

"But you're not convinced?"

"Not yet," I said.

"So, what's the deal about this bonding thing?" Allison asked again.

"I honestly don't know," I said.

"But you're going to find out?"

"Yes," I said.

We hung up and I thought about Russell and bonding and the streak of light in the sky and the blue aura master and shook my head...

I think I was still shaking my head when I finally pulled up to my house.

12.

"Anthony has a girlfriend, Mom."

I was in the kitchen, making dinner. Not quite as normal as it might sound. On a platter next to me were precisely fifteen grilled hot dogs. All for Anthony. And, yes, I had grilled them with my George Foreman. That's the way Anthony liked them, and it was easier than arguing with him. And, true to form, he wanted nothing on them. No buns, no ketchup, no mustard, no relish...nothing. Just fifteen Ballpark Franks, grilled, piled high.

Simmering on the stove next to me was Tammy's latest obsession. Chicken in yellow curry sauce. She'd gotten it into her head that she loved Indian food. Apparently, she'd had the stuff over at a friend's house, and now that's all she ever talked about...Indian food. And now, my kitchen smelled like, well, curry and garlic, with a beefy hot dog chaser.

The trouble was this: the hot dogs smelled heavenly...and so did the damn curry, although I never remembered liking Indian food before. It all smelled good. Heavenly, in fact.

At this point in my pitiful existence—anything, and I mean *anything*—would be a wondrous change to the every-other-day blood shots I took from sealed plastic bags that I popped open and gulped out of necessity.

Of course, I thought, *it didn't have to be that way, did it?*

No, it didn't. There was one more medallion out there, one more mystical talisman that had been created ages ago to help lessen the side effects of those afflicted with vampirism.

The diamond medallion.

Another such medallion was presently absorbed within my son. Yes, *absorbed.* Sounded weird, I knew, but my son had taken an alchemical potion that had contained the dissolved medallion. Somehow, the magicks within the medallion still flowed through my boy. Where and how, I didn't know. But one thing I did know was this...

I was a freakin' horrible mother.

I stopped stirring with this last thought and stared down into the simmering chicken and curry. No, I thought...not a bad mom. A desperate mom. I saved him, didn't I? My son was alive to this day, wasn't he?

He was, of course. In fact, he was in the living

room even now, watching *SpongeBob Squarepants* on Netflix. How the kid could watch those cartoons over and over was beyond me. But watch them he did, and often, all while laughing and giggling and slapping the floor hard enough to shake the whole damn house. In fact, these days, the house seemed to be shaking harder and harder.

No surprise there. The kid had shot up an inch over the last four months...all while filling out, too. He was only ten, but he now had the body of a high school football player.

Yes, I was a very, very bad mother.

I did this to myself often. I rarely, if ever, forgave myself. But I needed to forgive myself for doing what I did to my son—

For saving his life—

For turning him into a monster—

I paused, took a deep breath, collected myself, and then continued stirring the chicken and curry. Yes, my son had had some unforeseen side effects. But, I supposed, the side effects could have been a lot worse.

He could have been a true monster.

Of the blood-sucking variety.

And then a horrible thought occurred to me...one that I refused to entertain for longer than a few seconds before I beat it back into my subconscious...but here it was:

What if, someday, he did become a bloodsucker?

What guarantee did I have that he wouldn't just

keep getting stronger...but also more monstrous?

I didn't, of course. There were no guarantees in my world. A world that my son—and now my daughter—were now a part of.

No guarantees, yes, but there were answers...and I knew just where to go to find them.

The Librarian, I thought.

For now, though, I heaped a pile of steaming rice on a plate, covered it with chicken and curry, then stuck my head in the living room and told Anthony his hot dogs were ready. He nodded without looking at me and stood smoothly and effortlessly, all muscle and long limbs. I next headed down the hall and told Tammy her dinner was ready, too. She said she would come in a minute.

Anthony grabbed his hot dogs first, but I wouldn't let him leave without telling me thank you. He mumbled something utterly incomprehensible. It could have been a thank you. He also could have been having a seizure. I gave him the hot dogs anyway.

"Wait," I said. "What's this about a new girlfriend?"

He blushed mightily, which might have been cute. That is, of course, if we had been talking about anything other than a girlfriend. "She's just a friend, Mom. A friend who happens to be a girl."

Except he kept on blushing, his ears practically on fire, as he escaped back into the living room.

Next came Tammy. As with Anthony, I made

her say thank you before I gave her the food. Except, of course, she stared at me with defiance for exactly two minutes before hunger finally got the better of her.

"Fine!" she said, louder than was necessary. "Thank you! But it's your *job* to make us food, you know."

"Oh?"

"Yes."

"And what's your job?" I asked.

She grinned at me before exiting the kitchen with her plate of food. "To eat it. Oh, and Tisha is *not* a friend. Trust me on this one, Mom. I've seen them smooching." She made a kissing gesture that, quite honestly, I never wanted to see again.

A moment later, I heard her door slam shut, and I was left alone in the kitchen, with no food, and no real thanks.

Sigh.

13.

"So, why do you oversee such a creepy library?" I asked Archibald Maximus, the young librarian with the ancient name.

As usual, Maximus was been nowhere to be found when I had first entered the Occult Reading Room at Cal State Fullerton. I had rung the little bell on the counter and, after a moment or two, out walked the young man wearing nondescript slacks and a black long-sleeved shirt. He was handsome in a nerdy way.

"Someone has to," he answered. He stood on one side of the counter, his hands resting lightly on the counter itself.

"What does that mean?" I asked.

"It means that the knowledge in these books is not just for everyone."

"Who then?"

"Those ready for such knowledge."

"And you decide who's ready?"

Archibald leaned back against the wall behind him and folded his arms over his chest Archibald didn't have a lot of muscle tone. He had an average shape, perhaps even on the slender side. When he was done looking at me, and, probably, thinking about how to answer my question, he said, "I, and others like me, decide who may have access to such Reading Rooms. As for this particular collection, yes, I am the final gatekeeper."

"And what if someone demanded to have a book?"

"That someone would have a hard time finding me."

"What do you mean?" I asked.

"Look behind you, Sam."

I did, just as a student walked past, a young girl looking forward, oblivious to us. It was rare enough to see any students on this floor as it was, let alone catching one just as she passed by. Still, one thing seemed apparent.

"She didn't seem to notice us," I said.

"And she wouldn't, Sam."

"I don't understand. Are we invisible?"

"Not quite," said the Librarian, and he cracked a rare smile. A nice smile, and one that suggested he had seen a lot...perhaps far more than I would ever realize. "To those who have not earned the right to use this room—or, more accurately, who are not ready for this room, it is, shall I say, not on their radar."

"You mean they can't see it?"

"In a way. They would have to be drawn to it by a very strong reason, but, even then, they would have no interest in it, and would continue on. It is similar to those who hear a great truth. If the listener is not ready for the truth, it will fall upon deaf ears."

"But how was I ready to meet you?" I asked. "I mean, I'm no one."

The Librarian looked at me with compassion. "I've been aware of you for some time, Samantha Moon. Indeed, it was only a matter of time before we met."

"Geez. Who the heck are you?" I asked. Except I knew the answer to that. Archibald Maximus was, I knew, a great alchemist who had mastered life and death, albeit through alchemical means, rather than the alternative. The alternative being, of course, creatures like me.

"I'm not much different than you, Sam," he said with a smile.

"Do you have a highly evolved demonic entity living within you, waiting and plotting to take over your life?"

"Okay," he said. "Maybe we are a little different."

He smiled. I wanted to smile, but couldn't. Archibald was an immortal, and thus, his thoughts were closed from me, but, like the angel Ishmael, he seemed to have access to my own innermost thoughts...or perhaps he was an expert at body language, after all this time on Earth.

"But fear not, Samantha, for you are stronger than it."

"I don't feel stronger. I feel helpless."

"You are far from helpless, child," he said, and even though he looked years younger than me, his term of endearment touched me and I wanted to hug him tight and have him tell me everything was going to be okay. Whoever he was.

"Everything will be okay," he said. "If you allow it."

"Fine," I said, wiping my eyes. "And where's my hug?"

He came around the counter unhesitatingly, with open arms, and I slipped inside them easily and he hugged me tight and I felt his surprising strength and even his love—not a romantic love, and not necessarily a love just for me. His love seemed to radiate out, in a wide arc, encompassing, perhaps, the whole of mankind.

"Who are you?" I said again, into his shoulder.

He patted my own shoulder sweetly, as a father would. I wasn't sure anyone had patted my shoulder in a long time. The gesture was so comforting that I didn't want to let him go. It was, perhaps, the first time in many years that I truly felt safe.

"I am a friend," he said into my ear.

Finally, I pulled away shyly, wiping my tears. "Thank you."

He gave me such a warm smile that I nearly

hugged him again. Finally, he said, "I assume, Sam, that you came here to talk."

I nodded, taking a deep breath, getting a hold of myself. "No, I came for the hug."

He laughed.

"Okay, and maybe one or two questions."

He waited calmly. As he waited, I heard the familiar whisperings from deeper in the small reading room, a room that was crammed with every imaginable book on the occult and arcane, books on life and death and hidden histories, books on secret societies and black magic. Some books, I knew, opened doorways into other worlds, or worlds that were layered just over our own, worlds that sometimes crossed our path and interconnected. The whisperings, I suspected, were from these entities seeking entry into our world...and, I suspected, seeking willing hosts.

Like the creature within me.

She was a female, I'd come to discover. The sister to a powerful body-hopping demon that I had somehow managed to banish from an accursed family.

Now, from deeper in the Occult Reading Room, which, really, was just a few rows packed floor to ceiling with mostly oversized, darkish books, I heard something slowly, calmly, disturbingly calling out my name.

"Sssister," it said in a dry, raspy voice that seemed to be many voices speaking as one, voices that could have just as easily been my imagination.

"Sssister   Sssamantha...come   to us...waiting...waiting..."

"Ignore them, Samantha. They have no power over you."

"But *she* does," I said, tapping my chest.

"No. Not if you don't let her."

"But she already does," I said. "I can't eat normally, or go in the sun, or breathe or die or..."

He placed a hand on my shoulder. "I never said you had an *ideal* situation, Samantha. But she has not won, nor will she."

I nodded and wanted to cry. His touch did something to me...so comforting, so warm, so gentle...but I kept it together.

"I have two questions..." I finally said.

He waited, and this time I plunged forward, ignoring the beseeching whisperings from deeper in the room.

"Will my son...?"

Except I actually couldn't plunge forward. Not with Archibald Maximus looking at me so kindly, and not with the emotions that raged through me...from fear to fragile hope.

"Your son's condition was unexpected," said Archibald, perhaps tapping into my thoughts. "But, remember, your son did consume the ruby medallion. He will neither revert back into vampirism, nor can he be turned into a vampire."

"But is he immortal?"

"Immortality must stand the test of time."

"Is that a joke?"

"Not really, Sam. What it means, I do not know, and, I suspect, no one knows what will become of your son. But one thing is certain: he will never need to drink blood, nor will he ever shy away from the sun. The curse of vampirism has been lifted."

"But what is he?" I asked.

The Librarian's gentle blue eyes twinkled. He looked so much older than his smooth, handsome, nerdy face implied. "I suspect something very special, Sam. Now, I believe you have a second question about Russell?"

"Yes, how—never mind."

"Thoughts are vibrations, Sam," he said, answering anyway. "I don't so much read your mind, as read your vibrations."

"Of course," I said. "Doesn't everyone?"

"Everyone could, if they knew how."

"Then teach me."

"You are far better at it then you realize."

"Fat lot of good that does me." I gave him a small grin. I liked the Librarian, whoever he was. "Okay, here goes: can another human being be bonded to me?"

"In short, yes."

"Without them knowing it?"

"They know it, Sam. They allowed it. But, perhaps, they did not understand the full extent of the connection...and neither did you."

"Full extent of the connection?" I said, phrasing it as a question, mostly because I hadn't a clue what I was talking about.

"It means, he's devoted to you completely, and if coitus was involved, then the connection might be even deeper."

"Oh, don't get all puritanical on me now," I said. "You know very well we had sex."

"I might be many things," said Archibald, nodding slowly. "But one of them is not crude."

"Fine, whatever...just tell me what to do."

"You don't enjoy his devotion?"

"No...not like this. Not against his will."

"His will has allowed it."

"It's not right," I said.

"Good," said Archibald, and I suspect his last few questions had been a test of some sort. "Then you must release him, Sam."

"And how do I do that?"

"There's no correct way, I'm afraid."

"I don't understand."

"The connection between two people is deeply personal and intimate. You will need to find your own way through this."

"Great," I said. "Who makes this stuff up, anyway?"

Maximus grinned and leaned against the counter. "Oh, just us nerds."

14.

I recognized the girl.

Granted, this time she was lying on a slab of cold steel in the Los Angeles County Coroner's office. With me were Detective Sanchez and Dr. Mueller. The detective and I stood to one side of the mostly-covered body, while the medical examiner stood on the other.

Dr. Mueller wore a white lab coat that was mostly clean. There was a very faint splatter near his lapel. It was a fresh splatter...and it made my stomach growl.

Such a monster.

With that thought, Sanchez glanced over at me, alarm in his eyes. Our communication was open, as we had intended it. Sanchez and I had determined beforehand that a private, inner dialogue between ourselves wouldn't be a bad idea.

Don't worry, I thought to him now, *I can control myself.*

You had me worried there.

Trust me, drinking from stiffs in the morgue isn't my idea of fine dining.

That's disturbing on many levels.

Welcome to my world.

Sanchez didn't respond, but the look of *extreme concern* in his eyes said it all. Yes, I was a freak...so freaky that an armed LAPD homicide cop was nervous.

Not nervous, he countered. *Just...alarmed.*

Bullshit.

Okay, fine. You scare the shit out of me. In fact, I haven't been the same since we last met. I've been a nervous wreck and...

He paused, but I picked up his stray thought.

And you've been reading up about vampires? I asked.

Well, yes. Wouldn't you if you were in my shoes? I have to know more. I'm...so intrigued...and scared...but mostly intrigued. It's just so bizarre. I don't want you to remove my memory, Sam. I'll keep your secret. Just like Sherbet does. I need to know what I'm up against out here.

I looked at Dr. Mueller, who was staring at us from over his bifocals and waiting with, what I gathered, was extreme patience. I suspected that when you worked with corpses all day, you developed eternal patience.

Can we maybe talk about this later? I said to

Sanchez.

Yes, of course. Sorry.

Meanwhile, during our conversation, Sanchez and I had been idly scanning the body. My line of work didn't call for me viewing a lot of corpses. Neither did my job back when I was a federal agent for the Department of Housing and Urban Development, or the Office of the Inspector General. Back then, I mostly cracked down on fraud and waste and abuse in the various HUD programs. No, not very glamorous, but there were a lot of jerk-offs out there who were more than willing to scam the poor out of their life savings. Mortgage fraud and low-income housing went hand-in-hand, and I was proud to say that I had helped take my share of scumbags off the street.

So, with that said...no, not a lot of bodies in my chosen field. But I had also been recruited to help on other cases. The federal government did that sometimes. Grabbed agents from various departments to work bigger, more complicated cases. Or more important cases.

Yes, I had seen my fair share of examining rooms and corpses.

These days, death meant little to me.

I knew that was the result of the vampire in me, the killer in me, the predator in me...or *her* in me. She was trying to steal my humanity, my sympathy, to make me more like her, and less like the rest of the world.

Like the good Librarian had said, she didn't

have power over me.

Go away, I thought, wondering how much of me she could hear. *Go far fucking away.*

No, I had never heard her before, nor had I seen her or experienced her in any way, other than my enhanced powers and cursed affliction, all courtesy of her.

However, I had seen firsthand the evil that bubbled up to the surface when Kingsley had transformed into his hybrid form. Not to mention, just a few months ago, I had conversed and fought with perhaps the most powerful entity of all.

Her brother, in fact.

As I thought these thoughts, and as the good doctor waited for us patiently, I was very aware that Sanchez was staring at me again.

Not so cool anymore, is it? I asked.

Detective Sanchez said nothing, just glanced at me some more, then we both turned our full attention to the victim under the blanket. The stench of cleaning agents was strong in the air, scented ammonia and bleach being the predominant odors. Mostly, though, I detected another smell. The decay of rotting flesh. The victim wasn't in advanced decay, and so her stench wasn't very strong, but I could smell it clearly. Perhaps most disturbingly, it didn't bother me. Not at all. Perhaps most disturbingly, I thought I liked it.

Something is seriously wrong with me.

"Jesus," whispered Sanchez next to me, clearly picking up on my thoughts.

Scratch that last, I communicated silently to him. *I'm dealing with something here...something in me. Something I may or may not explain to you.*

He nodded, although he looked shaken, and not because we were standing over a body.

"Did you witness the autopsy?" I asked Sanchez aloud.

He nodded. "I did."

If the autopsy had bothered him, he didn't outwardly show it. Still, I sensed the mild revulsion ripple through him, and as it did so, I caught a brief glimpse of memory as he'd watched them use a bone saw around her scalp and lift out her brain.

He shuddered again. I didn't shudder. I was intrigued.

Lord help me.

I looked at the medical examiner, who was watching me with an eternal calm that might have made Half Dome in Yosemite envious. I said to him, "And what were your conclusions, Doctor?"

"She bled to death."

"May I see the wound in her neck?" I asked. There was a chance—a very small chance—that I might have asked this question a bit too eagerly. Sanchez glanced over at me again. I was making the poor guy nervous. Hell, I was making *me* nervous.

The doctor nodded and reached down and pulled back the sheet. The woman's face—a face I recognized from two nights ago, although that woman had been in a very different form—in spirit —was stapled back in place below her jawline. Her pretty face had been peeled back during the autopsy to expose the skull. Now, her face had been positioned mostly back into place, although it was slightly askew. I glanced at where some of the curled, unattached skin hung loose.

Fascinating.

Except, of course, I knew that I wasn't fascinated. *She* was fascinated...the thing that lived within me.

Freaky bitch.

The pathologist had us step around to his side of the examining table, which would have been the right side of the woman's neck. Yes, there was the gaping wound. I could see bruising and red, raw, hanging flesh. I noted the arched openings. Bite wounds.

"Looks human," I said.

"We believe so. We recovered human saliva along the opening, as well. The carotid artery was bitten clean through. She lost, precisely, half of her blood. Enough to bleed to death."

"One problem," said Sanchez, hovering somewhere above me. "We only found evidence of about a quarter of her blood."

"So, she bled elsewhere," I said, playing devil's advocate. Or, perhaps, the devil in me was just playing advocate.

Sanchez shook his head. "There's evidence that the attack took place on the trail, where she was also found. We didn't see any evidence that she was moved. We believe she bled to death where she was attacked."

"Except we're missing a quarter of her blood."

"Yes."

I glanced at the pathologist. "Are we being recorded?"

"No, the cameras are turned off. They're only turned on if someone wishes to view an autopsy from an adjacent room."

"From the safety of a TV monitor."

He didn't smile. Death was serious business. "Something like that. The smells can be a bit overwhelming at times."

That I was enjoying the smells, I kept to myself...and to Sanchez, who glanced at me again. I stepped closer to the medical examiner.

Can you hear me, doctor? I thought.

He cocked his head slightly, then nodded.

I'd learned last year that vampires can control others. To what extent, I didn't know. Truthfully, I didn't want to know. But something within me—the devil within me, I suspected—enjoyed controlling others. Needed to control others.

But I needed to now.

And I was enjoying every moment of it.

Good, I thought. *You are to destroy any evidence that links her death to a human. Your official report will state she died of an animal attack. We'll call it a rabid coyote. Understood?*

The good doctor stared at me from over his bifocals, then nodded.

Delete all computerized files and destroy all

written reports. Additionally, erase the cameras.

The doctor nodded again, and soon, Detective Sanchez and I stepped out of the laboratory and into the air-conditioned hallway.

To say that Sanchez was looking at me warily would be an understatement. "What happened in there?"

"We have to keep this on the down-low. You can appreciate that."

"No, I mean...all that creepy shit. You really enjoy death that much?"

"No," I said, answering truthfully. "She does."

"And who's she?"

"Another place, another time."

15.

We were sitting in Sanchez's squad car in one of Griffith Park's many entrances. I noted we were parked in a handicap spot.

Sanchez picked up on my observation, and said, "I'll move if it's needed."

"Good to know," I said.

We were one of a dozen or so other cars. A family of four was currently gathering blankets and an old-fashioned picnic basket. Their two young kids were kicking rocks at each other while the dad was texting, oblivious. The mother, of course, was doing everything, stowing the gear away and telling the kids to knock it off.

Typical. Moms are the true heroes of the world.

I want to wring the dad's neck and tell him to pitch in. To get off his goddamn phone and do something.

Then again, I was in a foul mood. Who wouldn't be? After all, for the first time since becoming a vampire—or whatever it was that I was —I'd really felt the influence of the thing living within me. Her desires were merging into my desires...and I didn't like it. I hated it, in fact.

And it scared the shit out of me.

Worse, I knew that she liked that it scared me...that she craved my fear, in fact. She fed off it. I suspected my fear made her stronger, braver, more audacious.

"Are you catching any of this?" I asked Sanchez.

"All of it, and I'm sorry. I mean, I don't know what the hell happened to you—or is happening to you—but it sounds pretty shitty."

"You have no idea."

"And this *thing* inside of you. Does it possess you?"

I looked at the handsome detective who filled the driver's seat completely. His hands were hooked over the lower half of the steering wheel. Big hands, squarish nails. The nails looked thick and healthy. All of him looked thick and healthy. Finally, I shook my head. "It's complicated."

"Try me, Sam. I'm a big boy."

I thought of burdening the detective with who I was, and what was happening to me. Why burden him and not Russell? What was the difference? I thought about that as the detective and I sat together in the dark car, at the base of a park where two innocent women had been slaughtered by a vampire, or a wannabe vampire.

The difference, I knew, was simple: Russell had never asked for any of this. The detective had a job to do, and part of his job included finding answers to two homicides. The answers just happened to be supernatural in nature.

Russell deserved answers, too. Since his girlfriend happened to be supernatural in nature, too.

"I know of Russell Baker," said the detective, picking up my thoughts.

"You follow boxing?"

"I do. He's a champion in the making." Sanchez studied me some more. "And I see he's bound to you in some way."

I chuckled. "You're getting pretty good at this mindreading thing."

"What can I say, I'm a natural. So what does it mean, bound to you?"

"I don't know yet, Detective. I'm still figuring that part out."

"Sorry, I ask a lot of questions."

"You're a homicide cop. It comes with the territory. And if I were you, I would be asking a lot of questions, too."

"If you were me, would you be afraid?"

"Are you afraid of me, Detective?"

"Back there, in the autopsy lab...yeah, I was a little."

"It's not me, Detective. It's her."

"Which comes back to my question: are you possessed, Sam?"

I almost laughed. "Now that's a question I bet you don't ask every day."

He smiled and waited. I felt suddenly sad and empty and lost. His eyes held compassion, but also wariness. That a grown man...that such a huge hunk of a grown man with a gun and his training and his muscles, would be wary of me, just made me realize all over again just how much of a monster I'd become.

"Not a monster, Sam. I just don't understand what's going on with you. Tell me about the thing within you."

"She's a highly evolved dark master."

"What does that mean?"

"Think of a highly evolved master—like Christ or Buddha. But she would be the opposite."

"She is evil."

"Perhaps," I said. "Although I'm not sure what evil means, exactly. I do know that she enjoys death. She enjoys taking life. She feeds on the fear of others. She enjoys creating fear. She enjoys, for instance, that you are wary of me. She wants me to exploit that. I can feel it within me. She hungers to control, to feed, to consume."

"Sounds evil to me."

"She does not see it that way. She sees it as a balancing of the light. A necessity."

"A necessary evil?"

"I think so, yes."

"Do you communicate with her?"

"No. Not yet. But she is getting bolder. I can feel her inside me more and more. I sense her impressions now. They filter up from wherever she resides."

"Sweet Jesus."

"The name alone makes her recoil."

"Interesting," said Sanchez.

"Very," I said.

"So, she doesn't possess you?"

"No. I am still me. But she influences me heavily."

"She is the source of your current powers?"

I nodded. "Or as some would have me believe, the source of my immortal condition."

"Why is she here? Why does she do what she does?"

"It is her entry into this world."

"Through you?"

"And others like me."

Sanchez blinked. "I just received an image of a hulking creature. Is that a..."

"A werewolf, Detective."

"You have got to be kidding me."

"I'm afraid not. Would you like for me to erase your memory now?"

"No. Not yet. Perhaps never. I need to know this stuff."

"Why?"

"I have a job to do, for one."

"You need to know what you're up against, and

all that?"

"Yes. But also..."

His voice trailed off, and I caught where he was going with this. "No, Detective. I can't let you."

"I want to help you, Sam."

I shook my head. "No. You don't know what you're talking about."

"Maybe I don't, but I know one thing, Sam: you need help. A lot of help. I may not be this big, hairy Kingsley fellow, but I have resources at my disposal, and I'm pretty good with a gun."

I chuckled...and as I did so, he sat back a little.

"Wait...Kingsley Fulcrum, the defense attorney...is a werewolf?"

"Does it surprise you?"

"He is a big-son-of-bitch."

"And hairy," I added.

"There is a lot of weird going on," said Sanchez, whistling lightly.

"I would say welcome to my world..."

"But it's my world, too," he said. "Now."

I didn't say anything about that, and as we sat here together, I focused on something that had been troubling me since I'd first met the LAPD detective in Sherbet's office.

"Tell me again why you first approached Sherbet?"

Sanchez looked at me, blinked, and as he did so, I noted something very curious in his memory. It was blank. He said, "You guys dealt with a similar incident. It seemed obvious to approach Detective

Sherbet."

Except, of course, I knew that the official records had been stricken of any connection that had anything to do with vampires. Officially, the murders taking place under the Fullerton Theater were the result of a serial killer. Unofficially, the murders were the result of a blood ring—mortals who supplied human blood to vampires. Any of that evidence had been destroyed and memories erased by another vampire named Hanner.

Sanchez, who had been following my train of thought, shook his head. "No, I remember reading something in the newspaper."

"Details of the crimes were not reported in the paper. Try again."

"I...I thought I had read it in the paper."

"The details of the crimes were covered up, Detective. Anyone and everyone associated with the Fullerton Blood Ring have been dealt with."

"What do you mean dealt with?"

"Memories altered."

"So, then, how did I know to call Sherbet?"

"That's the million-dollar question, Detective."

16.

Sanchez left me there at the park.

He didn't like it, but I told him it was part of my process. He had asked what process that was and I told him I hadn't a clue. He liked that even less, but he also sensed I wanted to be alone with my thoughts. And then, finally, I gave him a small glimpse of the creature that I would soon become.

"Holy shit," he said.

"That about sums it up," I said as I stood outside the driver's side door of his squad car. "Go home to your family, Detective, and forget about vampires and ghosts and giant flying bats."

"I couldn't if I tried."

"I could help you."

"No, please."

He gave me a lingering look, then looked out over the dark park, shook his head, then drove off, his tires crunching over the gravel parking lot.

I set off along the same trail, the same trail where a young lady had been killed recently, where she had bled to death. Where a quarter of her blood had gone missing.

Enough to feed a hungry vampire.

Perhaps even two.

***

The park was mostly empty.

Sometimes, I heard the rustling of smaller animals and the rarer mid-sized animal. Raccoons and skunks, mostly. Griffith Park was famous for its observatory and zoo and Greek Theatre, all of which have been featured in movies and TV shows ranging from *Rebel Without a Cause* to *Three's Company*.

Yes, we were directly above Hollywood, and Hollywood loved to film in its own back yard. Griffith Park was, quite literally, Hollywood's back yard.

I passed the crime scene again, and was pleased to see that the young lady's spirit was gone, although I saw residual energy, energy that would never go away. A murder scarred the land, perhaps forever. And what I saw, as I moved past that same boulder where I'd seen the ghost of the young woman sitting, was a chaotic collection of light that formed and reformed, swirling and dispersing, over and over again. Perhaps throughout all eternity.

Playing out the scene of her murder, at least at an energetic level, forever.

The world might forget this young jogger, but the earth never would. Perhaps this was its way of remembering the dead. Or not, I don't know. I was just a mom. Albeit a freaky mom.

I stepped into the frenzied energy, and, as I did so, I caught a faint feeling of fear, of pain, of confusion...and of excitement. The excitement was not from the victim. It was from the killer.

I paused on the trail, turning slightly, feeling the mass of energy around me. Psychics can tap into such energy, read it like a book. I was not a real psychic. Refer back to my mom comment. But I am real freaky, and sometimes I get psychic hits with the best of them. The hair along my arms and back of my neck prickled. I kept turning slowly, tuning in, locking in.

I knew the girl had no memory of what had happened to her. Her last memories were, in fact, a crazy mess of pain and fear and dying. Whatever had hit her, she couldn't see it, or never had a chance to see it.

My inner alarm system remained quiet. Whatever had been out here a few nights ago wasn't around now. Perhaps it was time to take another look around. So, I closed my eyes and reached out around me, expanding my inner sight as far as it would go.

I saw nothing human, although I saw plenty of glowing life forms, ranging from mice to a young deer. That I suddenly imagined myself pursuing the deer and feasting upon it might have had more to do with my recent viewing of the *Twilight* movies, than any bloodlust.

Still, I idly wondered what the deer's blood would taste like. Probably warm and delicious. I rarely, if ever, feasted on a living animal, and wasn't about to start tonight—Oh yes, I'd almost forgotten that time I had gone to a castle in Switzerland on a business trip and was accommodated, but I hadn't killed for my supper...someone had done it for me.

Try it, came a sudden thought. A very distant, faint, small thought at the far reaches of awareness. It sounded like my own thoughts, admittedly. Like something that had originated within me, but I knew, somehow, that it wasn't mine. It was too firm. Too controlling. Too evil.

It was her.

The entity that lived within me. I was sure of it, and it was, I was certain, the first time she had ever directly communicated with me.

I snapped back into my body, as a cold shiver came over me. The image of the grazing deer disappeared in a literal blink. I rubbed my arms and then my temples and wished like hell I hadn't just heard those two words. I wished like hell she would stay far away, or stay buried. I did not want to have to listen to her, too.

Indeed, hearing her now, her words rising up from the depths of my subconscious, hit too close to home.

Now she was pissing me off.

More importantly, though, hearing a second set of thoughts in my head, thoughts that sounded far too similar to my own, felt a bit like I was going insane.

As I stood there in the woods, feeling the scattered energy of a heinous murder around me, seeing animals I shouldn't see, hearing sounds I shouldn't hear, and hungering for something no sane person should ever hunger for, I knew I was fighting a demon of another kind.

My own personal demon.

No, I wasn't talking about her, the entity buried within me.

Ever since I first woke up in the hospital bed seven years ago, back when I first felt the changes coming over me, back when I first knew that I would never be normal again, I also wondered something else.

I wondered if I had gone insane.

At what point I had gone insane, I didn't know. Maybe I'd had enough of my kids fighting. Maybe I'd had enough of Anthony's skid marks. Or of Danny's cheating. Or of life itself. Maybe I had checked out long ago, mentally, that is. Maybe my mind was long, long gone.

And hearing a second voice in my head seemed to confirm that. Seemed to confirm my worst fears.

I didn't want to go insane. I didn't want to lose my mind.

I took a few deep, shuddering, worthless breaths...breaths that served no purpose other than to calm me down. Except the first few didn't do anything for me, but the next batch did. Finally, finally, I felt myself calming down. I reminded myself that I'd been hearing voices in my head for over a year now, ever since I'd first heard Fang's whispered thoughts.

This was no different, right?

But it *was* different. It was very different. Fang's thoughts sounded like Fang. I heard his inflections, his tone, his distinct voice inside my head.

These thoughts...

Well, these thoughts sounded like me. Just like me. As if they were my own.

Except, of course, they weren't.

Deep breaths, Sam.

Breathe, breathe.

Good.

Very good.

I turned in a full circle, hands on hips, breathing and calming down and saying anything I could think of to not lose it right here in the woods above Hollywood.

As I did so, as I calmed my mind, as I did my best to get something out of my head that might never leave my head—Lord help me—I found myself particularly tuned into the chaotic energy around me.

Most curious, I was tuned in holistically, from

seemingly everywhere at once.

I forgot about the voice in my head, the demon within me. I forgot that just moments earlier, I'd nearly gone into a full panic attack.

Instead, I saw the scene play out before me.

Not like a movie, exactly, but close. Perhaps a badly edited movie that jumped forward and backward in time, with a wildly swinging camera.

I saw her murder.

All of it.

***

She is running alone. I see this in real-time, as if it's happening now.

Panting, careful of her footing, looking at her wristwatch, looking up into the sky, clearly aware that it is getting late, clearly aware that she might be in a vulnerable position.

I see the shadow keeping pace behind her, too.

It is a smallish shadow. A lithe figure. Dressed all in black and wearing a hoodie. Tendrils of blond hair peek out, flap about.

She is moving far too quickly for human eyes to follow her, detect her. Except that a human's eyes aren't following her or detecting her. These are Nature's eyes. The land's eyes. Moving fast or slow, supernatural or not, it was obvious to me, as I stood there on the trail, tuned into the scene, that nothing escaped the eyes of Mother Nature herself.

The scene continued playing out before me:

The jogger is fleet of foot, stepping smoothly over roots and rocks, brushing past overgrown shrubs and through high grass. She pumps her arms rhythmically, breathing evenly through pursed lips.

She is unaware of the creature following, a creature that pauses every so often but keeps to the shadows.

A creature who undoubtedly assumed she was going undetected, unaware that her every movement was being forever recorded into the land, seared into the soil.

The female jogger hears something, and pauses, cocking her head to one side, and that's when her stalker attacks.

It's not pretty. It's violent and hard to watch, even for me. Especially for me. The force of the attack drives the girl to the ground. Something dark and shadowy and evil seems to be clinging to her. Not quite clinging...*attached*. The girl fights at first, but mostly, she screams, and soon she's not screaming anymore, but jerking violently, all while the little shadow stays on top of her, clinging like a hungry parasite.

It's over quickly.

I listen to the wet sounds of feeding and chewing and soon the little creature stands...and wipes the blood from her mouth.

This is the first time I get a clear look at the face inside the hoodie, a face that's illuminated by millions of particles of light.

I recognize her immediately.

I am most curious, however, at the identity of the person who's approaching from the shadows. Shadows that are alive with light, at least to my eyes.

A tall man is standing there, watching her, head cocked to one side.

I know him well, too.

17.

I was flying.

These days, I'd learned to pack my clothing into my pants themselves, tying off the whole shebang at the ankles like a makeshift duffle bag, all of which now dangled from one of my longish talons.

That I had a longish talon was still something I wasn't entirely used to, and if there was any upside to having something dark and evil living within me, this was it:

Flying.

Okay, kicking ass wasn't bad, either. I was stronger than most men—many men combined, in fact. Truth was, I wasn't entirely sure just how strong I was. I suspected I could channel—or perhaps funnel—whatever amount of strength I needed for any given situation.

And, if someone put a gun to my head (a gun

with silver bullets, of course), I would admit that being psychic and reading minds had its upside. So did having an inner warning system, which had alerted me many countless times to potential trouble...and saved my ass countless times, too.

As I flew over Griffith Park, beating my wings slowly, languidly, feeling the rush of wind on my face—or the creature's face I had temporarily become, I suddenly realized *why* I had such gifts. Why I was so powerful. Why I could fly and read minds and do all the crazy things I do.

These weren't gifts. No.

These were tools.

Tools to keep *her* alive. To keep her host healthy and viable. To keep me from dying off too quickly. So that she could grow stronger. So that she could plot and scheme.

Bitch.

Beneath me, the park gave way to the glowing dome of the Griffith Observatory, then over the Greek Theatre, then finally down along bustling Hollywood Boulevard. Yes, even from up here, I could see the Hollywood Walk of Fame, and its many brass stars embedded in the sidewalks. If I looked hard enough, I could even make out a name or two. In fact, I might have just seen Cher's.

Lucky me, I thought. Raptor-like vision and yet, as the creature, I could read.

Had anyone bothered to look up, they wouldn't see much. Just a shadow passing beneath the smattering of stars, briefly blotting out the celestial lights. Perhaps a stray strobe light might fall across me. This was, after all, Hollywood. But mostly, I was high enough and dark enough to go unnoticed, which I did, looking down at the mortals who went about their lives, idolizing stars, dreaming of stars, never guessing that something now flew among the stars themselves, directly overhead.

I banked to starboard and headed for the LAPD station, where I'd left my car earlier today.

As I flew, I turned my thoughts toward the person I had seen feasting on the young woman... and to the person I had seen step out of the shadows.

I had put off thinking about it.

I didn't want to believe it.

But I had seen him clearly. He was wearing his own hoodie, and his eyes glowed softly from within the dark depths. Not all vampires could see the flame just behind the iris. I could. Again, lucky me.

Fang's eyes had been glowing softly with twin flames of fire as he watched from the tree line. He did more than watch, of course. He soon came over and knelt next to the dead jogger, and when he lowered his face to her neck, I snapped out of the reverie.

But not before I'd seen Detective Hanner smile broadly, her lips coated with fresh blood. Another bitch.

I continued along, banking again and headed toward downtown.

Once there, I circled high above the police

station, wondering if I would show up on any radar, but doubting it. I found an alley not too far away, and dropped down into it.

Yes, there was a bum sleeping in it. No, he didn't wake up, even when a hulking, winged creature settled in next to him, a creature that I now knew was summoned briefly from an alternate world.

So weird, I thought, as I focused on the naked woman in my thoughts...the woman who was the real me.

She stepped forward, and I gasped, and the sensation that came over me was not entirely unpleasant. No, I didn't go through a physical transformation. My bones didn't break or elongate, and I didn't twist and writhe in pain, all of which, I was sure, made for good TV or movies.

I'd come to understand the process of transformation as the slipping into and out of existence, slipping into and out of this world and another.

And, naked as the day I was born, as I unwrapped my clothing, I suddenly wondered where, exactly, I disappeared to. Where did this body go?

If I summoned the winged creature from another place and time, did I, perhaps, switch places with it? I doubted it, but now I suddenly wanted to know.

Where did I go?

I would tackle that question another time.

For now, I had Fang on my mind, and in my heart. Seeing him again, even as he approached a murdered woman, even as he gazed down upon her dead body with hunger in his glowing eyes, brought back a very intense feeling within me.

I remembered just how much I'd loved him.

Lord help me, I loved him still.

18.

We were in bed together.

It had been a fun night. A sweet night. We had held hands and laughed and kissed. I needed this final, sweet memory, knowing what I was about to do, the heart that I was about to break.

I didn't know much about anything, but I knew that I couldn't live with myself knowing that another human being was supernaturally bound to me.

I don't want another bound to me.

I want them to love me, for me.

Russell was on his side, his warm hand flat on my stomach. Being a bloodsucker had done wonders for my body, but I was still a little curvy, yet still had a small stomach. I liked my stomach. Washboards were overrated and not very fun. Russell had a washboard stomach. In fact, he might have just been the hardest human being I'd ever touched. Yes, hard looked good, but wasn't very fun to snuggle next to.

Russell and I were still dressed. He had tried to undress me numerous times, and numerous times, I'd resisted. He didn't complain. He didn't get all whiny the way guys got when they didn't get sex. Instead, he lay next to me contentedly. I sensed a smile on his handsome face.

Sadly, it wasn't a natural smile.

It was a goofy smile that seemed oddly plastered on his face. It was a smile that reminded me of the body-hopping demon of a few months ago...but not evil. Russell's smile was goofy. Like a man hopped up on love.

But maybe that was too much to ask for. Maybe I didn't deserve love. Maybe it was selfish of me to love another, to bring them into my train-wreck of a life.

Yes, came a distant thought.

A thought, I was certain, that wasn't my own. It was her. Except it sounded so much like me. It could have easily originated in my own thoughts. It could have been my own. But it wasn't. This single word had been faint, distant, and slightly random.

It wasn't going to be easy to distinguish her thoughts from my own, but I had to. If I wanted to stay sane. If I wanted to keep myself from going crazy.

She was changing the rules.

Never before had she made a direct appearance

into my thoughts. Yes, her influence could be seen outwardly, by changing the chemistry of my body, the natural and supernatural state of my body.

But internally, she had stayed away.

Until now.

She was getting bolder, more brazen, more challenging. She had said "yes" just when I figured that I shouldn't love again. I didn't have to wonder why for long. Of course, she wanted me to feel lonely, to feel unloved, to feel less than what I was. And I knew the reason why. Low self-esteem, low self-worth were key components to her master plan. Most key was the absence of love. All of which made it easier to move in, to take over, to push me aside, or, perhaps, to remove me completely.

Love, I suspected, was the key.

However, I heard nothing further from her—thank God—and instead, turned my attention to Russell next to me, who was gazing at me even now with his big, round, puppy eyes. I could feel the love radiating from him.

No, not real love, I reminded myself. A *semblance* of love. Infatuation, perhaps. It was, in fact, a spell of some sort.

Very clever, I thought, directing my words to the thing that lived within me. *And shitty, too. Give me a feeling of love, a sense of love, a hint of love, and I confuse it for the real thing.*

When, in fact, it wasn't.

No, I was *controlling* Russell. I was *using* him for love. What he really felt for me, I didn't know.

But it wasn't real love.

Controlling others fed her. A lack of *real* love fed her. Low self-esteem and depression fed her.

All of which, I knew, would help her to eventually take control of me.

I'd seen what such a demon can do. I had watched her brother control an entire family.

I couldn't let that happen to me, ever.

Most important, I had to remove her.

Forever.

And it started with letting Russell go.

To sever his tie with me.

Except, of course, I hadn't a clue how to do it, and the Librarian had been no help.

No, he had been helpful.

He had said that I needed to find my own way through it, that the connection between two people is deeply personal and intimate.

I thought about that as I turned to my side and reached for Russell's hand. I opened my mouth to speak...and hadn't a clue what I would say...

19.

"Hi," I said.

"Hi, baby," he said, and squeezed my hand lovingly and with so much emotion that his grip literally shook.

Lord, help me, I thought.

"Are you okay?" he asked, and the exaggerated look of concern in his eyes was almost comical.

That's not him, I thought. The Russell Baker I knew was strong, confident, controlled.

The expression on his face suggested that his whole life, his whole existence, all of his happiness, hinged on my happiness. In fact, on my answer.

Lord, help me, I thought again.

"I love you, Russell," I started.

"I love you, too, baby, more than you know."

He tried to release his hand—except that I knew where that hand was going: to the first boob it could find.

Sex connected us beyond what was normal, what was healthy.

So, I held his hand firm and he relaxed it. He continued gazing at me with those big, beautiful, brown eyes. His muscles flexed and undulated just under his skin, like slumbering vipers. God, he was so sexy.

Not anymore, I thought.

Release him.

I considered telling him the truth, and then erasing his mind later. Yes, I could do that, but that wasn't fair to him, or his subconscious. I suspected that even if I did erase his mind that his subconscious would remember...and haunt him forever. Maybe not. Maybe he truly would forget. But I doubted it. His heart would remember. Somewhere, deep inside he would remember.

Was it fair to just break up with him, with no explanation?

No. He has to know, I thought.

It was the only way.

No lying. No hiding. Unfortunately for Russell Baker, I had been unaware of my ability to control him. Now I knew, and as I thought those words, tears came to my eyes.

The tears were for my heart.

And for Russell's heart.

Yes, I loved him. Yes, I thought there was a chance it was going somewhere.

But I will never control him, and would never

allow myself to control him. Or anyone. The bitch within me had effectively cut me off from loving another human, another mortal.

I had tried to keep Russell from the truth of who I was, but now the truth, I knew, would set him free. I swallowed and looked away as the tears continued to come to my eyes, knowing what I was about to, what I had to do.

Lord, help me, I knew what I had to do.

20.

It was after.

I'd spent the last two hours pouring my heart out to Russell, telling him everything, from my attack seven years ago, to my hunger for blood, to my supernatural abilities, to the love spell he was under.

At first, he had laughed lightly, holding my hand and wanting to change the subject. He tried to even have sex again. Then he tried to change the subject again. Then he asked me to stop. Then he asked why I was telling him all of this. Then he asked if I was crazy. Then he grew angry. He stormed out of the bedroom, only to return, rubbing his temples and pacing randomly.

He wanted to know why I was telling him all of this, why I was doing this to him, why I was pushing him away with my crazy talk. We had something good, he kept saying. Something beautiful and pure and real.

I got up from the bed and took his hand and led him through my house and into the garage. I had planned ahead for the night. The kids were with Mary Lou, and Russell and I had the house to ourselves. He liked that idea. He thought that meant a night of sex.

He thought wrong. Sex was the problem. Sex was binding him to me against his will. I suspected sex had this effect on many people, although perhaps not as strongly.

Once in the garage, I showed him the old refrigerator in the far corner. Dusty and dirty and forgotten—and also padlocked.

"What's this?" he had asked.

I said nothing, only fetched the key from under the old coffee can filled with random nuts and bolts, a can hidden behind a tool box on a shelf under the workbench Danny had made years ago. A workbench that never saw any work, since Danny had decided that chasing whores and neglecting his family was the best way to spend his free time.

I unlocked the refrigerator and pulled the door open. Inside was my latest shipment from the butcher in Norco. It was a simple cardboard box pre-filled with sealed packets of blood. The butchery had thought the blood was for laboratory experiments. At least, that's what Danny and I told them way back when, back when Danny had tried to be there for me. That lasted only a few years.

Danny had thought it was a good idea for the butchery to think the blood was for scientific purposes. I agreed. We used his name, and added a "Dr." in front of it. So now, all the packets and boxes are labeled: "Dr. Daniel Moon." A name I got to see every time I had the displeasure of drinking from one of these filthy packets.

"What's this?" Russell had asked.

"Dinner," I said. "Although these days, I have a human source."

Russell had been bending down, holding one of the malleable packets, which oozed between his long fingers. He looked up at me, the light of the refrigerator highlighting his scarred but handsome features. "What do you mean, a *human source*?"

I was leaning a shoulder against the refrigerator, arms crossed. I figured that if I was going to tell him the truth, then there was no holding back. "Allison Lopez."

"Your friend?"

"Yes."

"The psychic?"

"And, apparently, witch," I said.

He looked at me, then looked at the packet of blood some more. "This is blood," he said. "I should know. I see enough of it in my profession."

I nodded, waited.

"You really drink this stuff?"

"I do."

"Prove it."

I held out my hand and he slapped the packet

down in it. I used my naturally pointed nail to deftly slice through the plastic, as I'd done hundreds of times before. I held the clear packet up to him, which swirled with fragments of bone and hair and meat, and said, "Bottoms up."

I drained the packet quickly, fought the initial gag reflex I always felt when drinking the butchery-supplied blood, then showed him the empty packet.

"Holy shit," he said.

"That's about what it tastes like, too."

"But that doesn't prove anything, does it? Just that you, you know, like to drink..."

"Animal blood?" I said. "You think I enjoy this? That I have some twisted fetish?"

"I...I don't know."

I gripped his tee shirt and slammed him against the garage wall. He didn't have far to travel, maybe just a foot or two. Still, he hit the wall hard, which was fine. He could handle it. He was a big boy, a tough guy. Not to mention, the overgrown love bug needed some sense knocked into him.

Except he kept looking at me with that big, goofy, loving grin.

Granted, I *liked* the big, goofy, loving grin. It wasn't a bad thing to have a lover look at you this way. Except, in context, the look wasn't appropriate. If anything, Russell should have been nervous, or even afraid.

I'd just shown him a refrigerator of blood.

I'd told him my greatest secret.

He should have been running for the hills. Or

curled up in a big, muscular fetal position.

Not looking at me lovingly.

I lifted him off his feet, his shirt now ruined. "Stop looking at me like that, goddammit!"

Except he didn't stop looking at me like that. In fact, he looked down at me with even more love than ever. "I don't care what you are, Sam. I don't care if you're the devil himself. I love you. I will always love you."

"You should care, dammit."

And I didn't just drop him, but threw him as well. He went spinning and stumbling, slamming against my minivan, and ultimately skidding along on his bony ass. He was wearing sleek basketball shorts, and so he went skidding a half dozen feet.

"Why are you doing this, Sam?" he said, as I bore down on him, stalking him, hunting him. I had a sudden image of me pinning Russell down to the dirty concrete floor of my garage, burying my face in his neck, as I had seen Hanner do with the jogger.

I shook my head and fought off the image.

But it came again and again.

It was her, of course.

Tempting me.

She wanted nothing more than for me to pounce upon Russell, to feed from him, perhaps destroy him. She wanted nothing more than my own humanity to be destroyed in the process, to be abolished and removed. My humanity, I knew, was her greatest obstacle to coming forward. As long as I remained who I was, she would stay in the shadows. Must stay in the shadows.

But that didn't solve my present problem.

Russell, of course, being my present problem. A man who had become bonded with me, so much so that, even as I stalked him, he looked up at me with pure bliss. Pure love.

How did one erase the effects of a potent love spell? Or, perhaps more aptly put, a love curse?

I didn't know, but whatever I was doing, it wasn't working. I seemed to only be hurting him more. Confusing him more.

My instinct was to break him. To physically remove the love from him, to beat it out of him. To hurt him so much that he would never love me again. I knew this wasn't the monster in me. This wasn't *her*.

This was me.

But it wasn't right, and so I stopped before him, standing above him, my fists clenched as he looked up at me with hurt and confusion and, yes, more love than ever. Russell was a tough guy. He could withstand an onslaught, even from me. I would possibly permanently hurt him before I saw any change in him. He would take the punishment, and go on loving me afterward.

I stared down at him as he stared up at me. His shirt was torn. His knees were dirty from his tumble over the concrete of my garage. His big, beautiful, brown eyes were full of tears held in a sort of holding pattern. One good blink would send them cascading down his face.

That's when I felt my own tears running down my face.

All he knew was love, of course. He didn't understand what was happening. I wasn't getting through to him. Not on a conscious level. I needed to go deeper.

Whatever that meant, I knew I had to go deeper, break through the spell, to the real Russell beneath.

I dropped to the concrete next to him, sat cross-legged before him, and took both his hands...

21.

"I'm sorry," I said, squeezing hands.

"It's okay, baby. We all have our bad nights."

"Did I hurt you?"

"*You* hurt *me*?" He laughed.

None of this was right. We shouldn't be sitting in a filthy garage—which, by the way, I needed to rally the troops and get cleaned this weekend. The troops being, of course, Tammy and Anthony. Anyway, we shouldn't be sitting here in the garage. We should have been in bed, making love. Holding each other, falling deeper in love. And Russell was so easy to love, too. Russell was easy to be with...but now I know why. Everything was too easy. He was too amenable. There was no fight in him. At least, none left. Our relationship, I realized, wasn't real. It was built on the supernatural. The unnatural.

"Did you forget the part where I told you that I'm a vampire? That I drink blood? That you should want no part of me?"

He pulled me into him and tried to kiss me. I pulled back. He shrugged and kept on smiling. "Baby, I want every part of you."

"And don't you see how cheesy that sounds?"

"Baby, when it's love, there is no such thing as cheesy."

Okay, this had to stop, even if it was just to put a stop to the nauseating sweet nothings. I had to go deeper. I had to reach the real Russell.

"Will you do something for me, Russell?" I asked, still holding his hands.

"Anything for you, baby. You know that."

"I want you to close your eyes."

He did so instantly, without question, without hesitation. Had I been prone to, I could abuse his devotion to me, his bond to me. I could use him and abuse him and have him do my bidding, and that was exactly what *she* wanted me to do...the using and abusing would steal away more of my humanity, break me down further.

Such a bitch, I thought, and closed my own eyes.

I expanded my awareness out and around him. I wasn't going to control Russell's thoughts, not like I had done with the martial arts trainer last year, or the medical examiner recently. No, I was doing something different with Russell, something I had never done before, something that I wasn't sure could even be done.

I was looking for the real him.

Hi, Russell, I thought.

He jerked and opened his eyes. I didn't have to open my eyes to know this. Our psychic connection was strong, although I kept my own wall up, keeping him out of my own thoughts, as I had always done with him, never wanting to reveal to him my true nature, or just how freaky I really was.

I had wanted to build a real relationship.

Little did I know that I was controlling him more and more. In effect, I was inadvertently doing to him what the bitch wanted to do to me.

I couldn't do that. Not to Russell, not to anyone.

"Is that you?" asked Russell. "In my head?"

I nodded and thought: *Yes. Now close your eyes, Russell. And keep them closed and focus on my words.*

"Okay," he whispered.

His hands, I noted, were shaking. A part of him was scared. That part of him was not allowed to surface, hidden beneath the spell, no doubt frightened and lost and confused as hell.

I literally felt myself slip into the flow of his thoughts. They were not jumbled, as many thoughts were. Indeed, poor Russell's thoughts were a steady stream of love flowing toward me. I had to admit, that felt nice. What girl wouldn't want her man to think such thoughts?

But they weren't natural.

I dipped into these loving thoughts, reveled in

them briefly, and pushed forward...and downward.

I'd never slipped this deeply into anyone's thoughts. Never thought I had to nor would want to. In fact, I had doubted I could. But sex did wonders, connecting two people deeply...perhaps deeper than they realized. Certainly deeper than I had realized.

After my attack, Danny and I had never had sex again. Maybe that had been a good thing. After all, he would have been bound to me like a lovesick puppy. Then again, he probably wouldn't have cheated on me, either, and my family would have remained intact.

But that would have been controlling, and I wouldn't have learned his true scumbag nature.

Russell wasn't a scumbag. At least, I'd never seen evidence to the contrary. Then again, within a few weeks, we had gotten intimate, and, perhaps, the spell had begun then. So, again, I wasn't seeing the real Russell. Perhaps I never had.

No, I had seen the real Russell in those first few weeks: strong, jovial, confident, driven, and sexy as hell.

Down I went through Russell's thoughts, deeper and deeper. And the deeper I got, the more chaotic they got, too. Gone was his undying love for me. Here were thoughts about boxing, working out, the death of Caesar Marquez. There were thoughts about me, too— wondering what he felt about me, wondering if we really had something here, wondering why I always felt cold, wondering why I never ate, wondering why I was so pale, wondering why he couldn't see a section of my face when we had walked past a mirror, wondering why I was so strong, wondering why I only slept during the day. These were his normal thoughts, and they were thoughts from many, many months ago.

Russell was in a sort of holding pattern, I knew. Which made sense. He hadn't fought for three months now, and he rarely worked out.

He had been, of course, focused on me, while the rest of his life was forgotten.

Yes, I had to stop this. Now. Despite the heaviness in my heart. Then again, perhaps what I felt for him wasn't real, either. His sweetness, kindness, and attention was all a sham. It was all spurred on by a spell.

No, he *was* sweet. I'd always remember the quiet, confident boxer who first came into my office and hired me last year.

I went deeper still, slipping beyond phobias and fears and secret sexual desires. I paused briefly at one, raised my eyebrows, and then continued down deeper into his subconscious.

How, exactly, I did this, I didn't know.

But I saw it almost as a physical journey, flying down through the various layers of his consciousness. I knew I was sitting in the garage, in dirt and oil and filth, holding his hands, eyes closed, but I was on a surprising journey through another person's consciousness.

But I still hadn't reached the *real* Russell Baker.

I passed through some of his oldest memories,

and down into his early childhood. I watched him both picking fights and being picked on. Those who picked on him soon found themselves in a lot trouble. I almost laughed as I watched him single-handedly beat up two bullies.

Down I went. Deeper and deeper.

Early childhood memories. A loving mother. An asshole father. The father beat him, but Russell always fought back.

Deeper and earlier, and soon I saw something rather amazing. Burning brightly in his deepest memories was a furious ball of white light. Hovering there in his thoughts.

Waiting for me.

Two words appeared in my mind: *Hi, Sam.*

Russell? I thought.

But, of course.

22.

I smiled, although I kept my physical eyes closed.

Yes, this sounded like the real Russell. Confident, humorous, carefree. Not obedient, agreeable and, well, love-struck.

I did fall in love with you, Sam, but something funny happened on the way to the Forum...

You fell under my spell.

I sensed him chuckling. *Something like that.*

So, who am I speaking to, exactly?

It's me, Sam. The Russell you met and remember, I'm just sort of...buried down here. Watching myself from a distance, watching myself act like a love-starved schoolboy. That's some spell.

The ultimate pussy-whipped spell, I thought, and blushed, although I didn't think Russell could see me blush. I was still talking to his ego. The part of him that was him. Not his higher self or spirit.

He laughed lightly in my head. I was still looking at a very bright spot...what this was, I wasn't sure. Perhaps his focused energy. Or perhaps this is what the mind looked like at its deepest, most unreachable spot.

Unreachable by most, Sam. Not you, apparently.

So, you believe me now? I asked. *That I am, you know...*

A vampire?

Yes, I thought.

You have a hard time saying it, don't you, Sam?

Yes, I thought. *I do.*

Why is that?

Because it's crazy. I can only handle so much crazy.

You're in denial, Sam.

Oh, yeah? And what do you know of vampires?

Not much, but it's pretty obvious you are one.

That obvious, huh?

I knew something was up by our third or fourth date.

What gave me away?

Your skin, mostly. You were always so cold.

But I used hand warmers!

Russell laughed, the sound reaching me distantly. *True, but the rest of you was always so cold. Your cheeks, your lips, your shoulders. And I mean cold. Ice cold. Dead cold.*

Ouch, I thought.

There are no secrets here, Sam. We're both an open book. At least, I am. I can see that your mind is still closed.

You know more than I give you credit, I thought.

We all know more than we give ourselves credit for. The problem is, there's too much surface shit that gets in the way, too many clouds obscuring our thoughts, filling us with worry and doubt and fear. It stops us from tapping deeper within ourselves.

Good to know, I thought. *But I have a hard time believing you could ever be afraid.*

You would be surprised, Sam. For instance, I'm afraid now.

I caught his meaning. *You are afraid that you might never come back.*

Yes, Sam.

How do I release you? I asked.

You're doing it now.

And how, exactly, am I doing that?

By reaching out to me, connecting to me, bringing me out of the funk I was in.

You call this a funk?

It's the funkiest of funk, Sam. Limbo, actually. A dull state where days and weeks and months slip past, and I can only watch from a distance, watching as I act like a love-struck fool.

But you love me, too.

I do, Sam.

I'm sorry I did this to you, I thought.

It wasn't your fault, Sam. I believe you didn't know what would happen.

I wanted to bury my face in my hands, to hide the tears that had started to come, but I needed to hold tightly to Russell, to keep the connection.

Had I known, I thought, *I never would have let things get as far as they had.*

I know, Sam. I also know that you have total control over me. I am, quite literally, at your mercy. You could do with me as you wish. I would do anything for you. Or, rather, the cursed part of me would do anything for you.

The love-struck schoolboy?

Yeah, him.

I don't want to control you, Russell.

I know you don't, Sam.

But you need to know that there's a part of me that I struggle with, a part of me that does want to control you. To use you, to make you do...

Your bidding? he asked lightly, laughing.

Yeah, that.

We all have our inner monsters, Sam. Yours is just a little more obvious.

I had given Russell a glimpse inside of me, of what I dealt with, and he had obviously sensed the demon within, the demon waiting to come out.

I'm sorry you have to deal with this, Sam.

Thank you.

But there's one thing I do know above all else.

The tears were really flowing now. I felt them running unhindered down my face, into my sweatshirt.

I know that you will beat her, Sam. You will

beat the shit out of her, too.

That's just the boxer in you, I thought, and nearly laughed.

Maybe, he thought. *But I also know this. There comes a time when we all have to stand up for what we believe. There's a time for love, and a time for war. And your time for love is not now, Sam. Your time for war is now. Get her, Sam. Remove her and beat her back to wherever she came from.*

And what of love? I thought, weeping silently.

Not now, he thought. *And not with me, Sam. Not ever.*

I buried my face in my hands, letting go of his own.

Release me, Sam, I heard him say from somewhere deep in my thoughts, his voice fading, now barely discernible. *Release me...release me...*

23.

Russell was gone.

I felt empty and alone and unlovable, almost suicidal. Almost. I would never leave my kids or my sister or Allison or any of my friends. No, not over lost love. But as I sat there at my kitchen table, my head in my hands and a cup of lukewarm tap water in front of me, I felt as if something very precious had been stolen from me.

Stolen by *her*.

The ability to love and be loved romantically.

I fought more tears, then decided not to fight them and let them flow and shook my head and cursed her and God and the Librarian and myself. I cursed the vampire who had first attacked me. I cursed Fang because I was pissed off that he left me. I cursed Kingsley for cheating on me, and cursed my ex-husband for abandoning me when I needed him the most. I cursed the stupid glass of water in front of me and the filthy blood in my freezer in the garage. I cursed my unattached garage because who buys a house with an unattached garage? My cheap ex-husband, that was who. So, I cursed him some more. And cursing him felt the best of all, and so I did that for a few more minutes until I couldn't curse anymore and couldn't see through the tears. I picked up the glass of water and threw it across the kitchen, so hard that it shattered into a million pieces and put a hole in a cupboard. I cursed the million pieces.

And then I was done cursing. I just sat there and wept, my mind empty. And later, when I was done weeping, I thought of one person. The person I missed most of all. Not Kingsley or Russell and certainly not Danny.

I thought of Fang.

I missed him so much that I thought I would scream.

And then I did scream.

Loudly.

So loudly that a dog down the street started yowling along with me.

24.

After I had cleaned up the glass, I made a mental note to call a handyman. I might have been able to fly to the moon and back, but I sure as hell couldn't fix something like this.

As I sat back at the kitchen table, I got a text from Anthony. It was a close-up picture of his nose. Actually, it was a picture of the *inside* of his nostrils. It was kind of blurry. Under the picture were the words: *Miss you, mama!*

I wrote: *Miss you, too, now go to bed.*

Boo, he wrote. Then added: *"ger"*

Yes, booger. Go to bed. Tell your sister I love her.

Better yet, I would. I texted her cell phone directly, telling her I loved her and missed them. Her response was immediate: *Anthony's annoying me.*

That's all you have to say? I wrote back.

Well you know I love you, mom! Do I always have to tell you????

Yes.

Fine!! I love you! Better?!!?

Yes, so much better.

Gawd!!

I told her to go to bed, too, to which I didn't receive a reply back. I sighed and turned my ringer off for a few minutes and got up from the table, found a pad of paper and a pen in my messy utility drawer, and sat back down.

I took in a lot of air, held it for a few minutes then expelled it slowly. I did this again and again, clearing my thoughts, ignoring my troubled heart. I continued doing this until I felt my hand jerk slightly. Followed by my whole arm, the pen began to move across the blank page as if on its own.

Three words appeared on the page before me: *Good evening, Samantha.*

"Is this Sephora?" I asked aloud.

My hand jerked some more. *Yes, Samantha.*

"It's been a while since we last spoke."

Yes.

"Does that bother you?"

I am here for you, Samantha, as I will be until time immemorial.

"You have nothing better to do?" I asked. It was meant as a flippant joke, but it came across as sort of rude even to my own ears. "Sorry," I added. "Didn't mean it that way."

My hand jerked, coming alive with small impulses of electricity. I watched in mild amazement all over again as my hand wrote seemingly independent of me.

You are the better thing for me to do, Samantha.

"Now, that was a sweet thing to say," I said. In fact, those words were exactly what I wanted to hear. I nearly broke down at their kindness, even though I wasn't sure who or what Sephora was. But I powered through, fighting back the tears...after all, I had cried enough for the night.

A kind word goes further than you think, my hand wrote on its own volition.

"I've heard that," I said. "The Ripple Effect."

Kindness is kindness, Samantha. It's not a theory or an effect or a movement. It just is.

I thought about that, and I thought about the bitch living inside of me, the demoness, as I thought of her.

"And what of her?" I said, knowing that Sephora knew my innermost thoughts, suspecting she was as close as I got to a guardian angel these days, since my own guardian angel abandoned his post nearly two years ago. "Do I show her kindness, too?" I added. "Perhaps let her take me over for all eternity, while I watch from the shadows, a prisoner in my own body?"

It is a grim picture you paint, Samantha.

"It's a grim reality," I said. "And, for the love of God, please don't tell me to choose a new reality."

I won't, Sam, especially since you summoned in

the love of God.

"Is that a joke?"

An observation. Love is a powerful tool. In fact, it's your only tool.

"To beat her?" I asked.

To help her, Sam.

I blinked in the darkness, which wasn't really darkness. All around me, like sunlight sparkling on ocean waves, glittered flashes of radiance. As always, within the radiance, I could see anything and everything.

I blinked again, and said, "Help her how?"

To move on, Sam.

"Move on to where?"

There was a long pause and my hand remained motionless, finally I felt the tiny electrical impulses and watched as my hand spelled out a single word: *Home.*

And just as the word appeared, I heard a small shriek in the back of my mind, deep beneath my many layers of consciousness. It was *her*. And following that faint shriek, I saw an image of a bright soul being absorbed by a much brighter light.

"She's showing me an image," I said, not liking this at all, not liking that she could leak images to me now. Yes, she was growing bolder and more powerful. I swallowed and said, "At least, I think it's her. She's showing me a soul—hers perhaps—being absorbed by a much bigger soul...or by something eternally big. God, perhaps."

Yes, Sam, my hand wrote, *she will be returned*

to the Creator.

"I don't understand what that means."

This question was followed by silence. In particular, my hand remained motionless.

I added, "You don't know what that means, either."

No one does, Sam. Not exactly.

"Is it a bad thing?"

Never. It's a loving thing. A loving process.

"At least, you think it is."

She will be returned to the Creator...who created you and me out of love.

"I see lots of people around me who are not very loving."

You see lots of people who are growing, Sam. Evolving.

"Meanwhile, they hurt others, terrify others, and wreak havoc upon the world."

These lost souls are not as abundant as you are led to believe, Sam. Remember this: there is more good than bad.

"But there is bad."

There is also confusion, anger, hate and misery, all of which can drive good people to do bad things, temporarily.

"So they are not really bad. They are bad in the moment."

Bad is relative, Sam.

My head was hurting, which was saying something since my head almost never hurt. And, like the true freak I was, the pain in my head went away almost instantly. I said, "What's bad to one person..."

Is justice to another, or fair to another, or right to another.

"But there is evil in the world?"

There is only light and dark, Samantha.

"Then who or what is in me?"

There was a long pause before my hand twitched and twitched, and the words it spelled out left me sick for the rest of the night...and it wasn't the kind of sickness that my immortality could heal.

Perhaps the darkest of them all.

25.

I was alone in bed.

Dawn was coming. I knew this because I could feel it coming in every fiber of my being. It wasn't a good feeling. In fact, it made me nervous, agitated. Now I knew the reality behind the feeling. Sunlight made *her* nervous and agitated. The demoness within.

And Fang wanted this? I thought. *Fang sought this?*

I shook my head and clawed at my covers, restless as hell, agitated as hell. My kids were still with my sister, as they often were during the summer. She took them willingly enough, knowing my penchant for working the late shift. I think she also wanted to give them a normal home, even if for a few hours a night. She hadn't said so in so many words, and, truthfully, I didn't blame her. In fact, I was okay with it. A few times a week with her was okay by me, especially during the summer.

Yes, I had missed a golden opportunity to dig deeper into the murdered jogger case tonight, but I had needed my time with Russell. It had to be done, and now was the time.

And now, of course, he was gone.

Would I ever see him again?

A part of me thought no. A part of me thought my handsome, young, sexy boxer with the bad-boy tattoos was forever gone.

I loved him, yes. But our love had never had time to mature. Too soon, it was stunted and distorted by the curse. I had not gotten to know the *real* Russell, and now, I never would.

Yeah, I moped around most of the night, depressed, pissed, agitated, slightly sick to my stomach. The blood packet I had downed had too many impurities in it. Enough to make me slightly sick.

But now, the need for sleep was coming hard. I was presently in stage two of three, of what I thought of as my before-sleep countdown. Stage two meant that I damn well better be near a bed, and in a dark room. I suppose a casket would work, too, but how weird was that?

"Too weird for me," I whispered into my pillow.

The entity within me was silent, as she usually was. What provoked her into contacting me recently, I didn't know. And whether or not she was truly getting stronger, I didn't know that either.

But I suspected she was, and I thought I knew why.

Her strength had been building over the years, but not because of time itself. I added to her strength each time I lost a little more of myself. Sephora had hinted at it.

No matter what, at all costs, I had to retain who I was and not let the vampire in me consume me completely. If so, she would win. If so, I might not ever return.

I did not want to spend an eternity on the sidelines, watching the thing within me ruin and destroy lives.

With that thought, as the rising sun approached on the distant horizon, not quite dawn but only minutes away, as I slipped from phase two into phase three, I thought of Detective Hanner, my one-time vampire friend.

How far gone was she? I knew Hanner had killed without remorse or discrimination. She had personally run a blood ring, overseen by psychotic killers. And I had watch her kill the lady jogger.

As Fang stood by and watched...

And then joined her.

Yes, Hanner was very far gone, although, I suspected, not entirely consumed by the darkness within her. And, with sudden clarity, I suspected I knew why.

"She made an agreement with it," I said sleepily to myself.

I nodded into my pillow.

Yes, that was it, of course. She had made an agreement with the entity early on. By allowing it to surface, to briefly possess her body, to live in this world sooner rather than later. By doing so, it, in return, gave Hanner access to her own body.

Kind of it, I thought.

Well, I wasn't making a deal with the bitch within me. She wasn't going to surface. Not now, or ever.

"You can go to hell," I mumbled aloud, barely coherent.

And, just before sleep hit me, I knew what I had to do.

I had to find Hanner...and Fang.

26.

I was in my minivan.

Driving along the winding Bastanchury Road through the back hills of Yorba Linda, on my way to see an honest-to-God werewolf and a butler who may or may not have been Frankenstein—yeah, no shit—when my cell phone rang.

Restricted. I.D.

It was either Detective Sherbet or Detective Sanchez, so I played it safe. "Hi, Detective," I said.

"How did you know it was me?" asked Sanchez.

"Lucky guess," I said.

Our connection wasn't so strong that he could read my thoughts long distance, which was a good thing, because he might have known I wasn't quite so awesome. *Can't have that.*

"We have another body, Sam."

My smug grin faltered. "Where?"

"Same place, same trail. Griffith Park."

"Who?"

"A park ranger this time, which means this is about to get ugly fast."

"Griffith Park has park rangers?"

"Apparently so. Look, rangers are cops in their own right, and there's going to be a lot of questions about this one. A lot of people are going to want answers."

He was right, of course. Park rangers were cops, too, and when one of their own went down, well, whole departments—hell, whole agencies—kicked into gear.

"Officially, it's going down as a cougar attack."

"Good," I said. "Leave it at that. Fight for that. Don't let anyone suggest otherwise."

"Sam, the wound is identical to the jogger. We can't hide this for long."

"You won't need to," I said.

There was a pause. I swear to God, I thought I might have even heard his heart beating through the phone. Maybe our connection was stronger than I'd thought. "What do you know, Sam?" he asked.

I shielded my thoughts of Fang. "I can't tell you. Not yet."

"Do you know who did this?" asked Sanchez.

"I do."

"Tell me, goddammit. I will personally hunt these fuckers down—"

"And that's the problem, Detective. I don't know where they are or what's going on, or why they're killing the way they're killing."

"They?"

"There's two of them."

"Are they like you?" asked Sanchez.

"They are just like me," I said.

"What's your plan?"

"I'm going to find them," I said. "And stop them."

"How?" he asked.

I aimed my car into Kingsley's long-ass drive-way. "Any way I can."

27.

Franklin the butler answered the door.

As usual, he gazed down at me from high above his long nose. That his ears were two different sizes —and two different color tones—was something I was almost getting used to. Almost. That the ears were not quite level was another matter.

"Master Kingsley is...indisposed," said Franklin.

"Indisposed, as in, with a woman?"

"Indisposed," Franklin intoned irritably, his enunciation impeccable, with a slight British accent. And something else, too. French perhaps.

I was surprised to discover that I felt mildly jealous at hearing these words. I brushed past the big butler, touching him for the first time, my hand on his shoulder. As I did so, I couldn't help but notice the fact that he was hard as a rock...and just as immovable. Good thing there was just enough

Samantha Moon space between him and the door frame.

"Well," I said from the foyer, as Franklin turned slowly and scowled at me. "Then I shall wait in the sitting room until Kingsley is *un*-indisposed."

***

Footsteps.

Two sets of them. One barefoot, one heeled. The barefoot ones sounded like two slabs of beef slapping against the tiled floor. The heeled ones sounded a little too cute and spunky for me. The footsteps wound down the spiral stairs, then through the hallway, then over to the front door. At the door, there were whispered words spoken. I couldn't quite make them out—didn't want to make them out. Still, my hearing was kind of awesome, if not superhuman. So I did catch a too-sweet "See you soon" followed by sounds of lip smacking. *Eww.* Finally, mercifully, the door opened and the sounds of clicking heels faded away, cut short by the shutting door.

More sounds of bare feet slapping, and a moment later, Kingsley stood at the entrance to the sitting room.

"This couldn't wait?" he asked.

"I waited," I said sweetly.

"Franklin came to the bedroom at a, um, crucial time."

"Gee, I'm sorry," I said, equally sweetly. I

might have batted my eyelashes once or twice. "Did I throw off your rhythm?"

He growled from deep within his throat and swept into the room, his silk robe fluttering open, briefly flashing me. I nearly wretched...knowing where that *thing* had just been. He smiled slyly at my reaction and sat across from me, exposing himself once again as he crossed his tree-trunk-like legs.

"Did you at least shower?" I asked.

"I didn't have a chance, Sam. You see, Franklin came to my door and said that you were here waiting. That it was important. You think I would waste precious time showering when something is so important?"

"I've been waiting twenty minutes."

"I asked if you thought I would waste precious time showering, not finishing."

"You're a pig."

"I am, but you knew that when you first met me."

It was true. Kingsley had been an infamous womanizer back when he'd hired me two years ago. I'd made an honest man out of him; that is, until my fallen angel had decided to show me Kingsley's true colors...and baited my then-boyfriend. Kingsley had fallen for the bait, and screwed his way out of our relationship. He had been trying to win me back ever since.

He laughed lightly, got up again—this time, mercifully keeping his robe closed—and went over to the bar in the far corner of the room and poured himself a finger or three of Scotch. He next reached into the wine cooler and removed what I could only imagine was a fine bottle of white wine—a chardonnay, no doubt. He poured a healthy amount, recorked it and returned the bottle to the fridge—knowing I generally only drank one glass.

"Ferrari-Carano," said Kingsley, coming over to me and handing me the cool glass. "Your favorite."

It was, although a fat lot of good it did me, since I hadn't been buzzed in seven years. At least, not buzzed on alcohol.

"Thank you," I said, "and thank you for flashing me for a third time."

"Third time's a charm," he said, making himself comfortable on the couch across from me.

"More like three strikes and you're out," I mumbled.

"I heard that, Sam. My hearing's a little better than yours."

"That's right, because you're part dog."

"Sam..."

"Or, should I say, *all* dog?"

"Sam, I've apologized for what I've done."

"Then apologize again, dammit."

He looked at me from over his amber-filled glass. His bare foot waggled nervously, like a dog's tail. His shaggy hair hung disheveled around his shoulder. He gave me a sincere look. It was the same look, I was willing to bet, that he'd given jurors in courts of law. Still, he was trying, and I appreciated his effort.

"Sam," he said, "I'm truly sorry that I did what I did. It was stupid mistake."

"Damn right it was stupid."

"I was stupid."

"Damn right, you were stupid."

"Now, other than getting on me for the hundredth time about my stupidity, why did you come here tonight?"

I wanted to still be mad at him, but how did I stay mad at a werewolf who wiggled his foot like a puppy dog who needed attention? I couldn't, and let it go for now, and I told him about my new case. He listened quietly, drinking idly, nodding sometimes and making wolfish grunting noises. Okay, maybe not wolfish. That might have been my imagination.

When I was wrapping up, I added, "You know Hanner, Kingsley. And you knew her well before I did. Hell, she supplied you blood for me...or for your other vampire guests. I need to find her."

"I don't know much about her, Sam. In fact, I would hazard to guess that you know far more about her at this point than I do."

"How did you two first meet?" I asked. I was holding my wine, but it was mostly forgotten. Little things like my throat getting dry or my voice getting hoarse from too much talking never, ever happened to me these days. Minor irritants like that healed instantly. And my body, apparently, didn't need much water. I knew water helped remove dangerous toxins from normal people. Except, of course, I had no more fear of dangerous toxins of any sort. I knew water cushioned joints and helped carry nutrients to cells and helped regulate body temperature.

What, exactly, was cushioning my cells, I didn't know. And whether or not my cells needed any nutrients, I didn't know that either, but one thing I did know was this: blood did the universal trick. It had everything I needed, and then some. I'd gone days without drinking water and hadn't missed a beat. And, no, I didn't use the bathroom, either.

Like I said, I'm a freak.

Yes, I operated by different physical rules, although the emotions had mostly stayed intact. I could still feel hurt and jealousy and rage. Losing control of myself was just what *she* wanted. I had to stay in control. Stay human.

"We met at a paranormal convention," Kingsley was saying. "At the North Pole with Santa Claus."

"Jerk," I said.

He chuckled lightly. "Sam, I'm involved in a sort of network of the undead, you could say. Or, in my case, supernaturals."

"You are not undead?"

"Not quite, Sam. I can live for a very long time, but werewolves are not ageless."

Kingsley had explained once the reason for his great size. He had not started out so big. Over the years, and with each cycle of the moon, his body adopted the werewolf's form more and more. The bigger he got, the closer he got to the beast within, the easier it was for him to transform with each full moon. A change that was not very pleasant.

I nodded. "If werewolves were immortal..."

"We would be big as cars," he finished.

I recalled the hulking beast standing in my hotel room two years ago. Yes, Kingsley was huge in his changeling form. Truth was, he was not that far off from his alter ego's size.

"How old are you again?" I asked.

"I'm close to eighty, Sam."

"And you don't look a day over forty-five."

"I was thinking forty, but whatever," he said. "And I know what you're thinking..."

I looked at him for a long moment, and fought a strong need to reach for his big hand. "What am I thinking?"

"You're wondering how I could possibly be so good looking. It's not easy, let me tell you. The hair care products alone cost me a fortune."

I laughed, and as I did so, I realized there would be a day when Kingsley wasn't here for me either, and that thought brought anguish to my heart and tears to my eyes.

"Hey, kiddo," he said, reaching over and gently lifting my jaw. "I'm not going anywhere for a long time."

"How long?"

"A long, long time."

I nodded and briefly hid my face in my hands. I guess I cared about Kingsley more than I realized. No, I had always cared about him. Our timing hadn't been right. Not initially, when I was dealing with a cheating spouse. And just when my heart was healing, just when I was coming around to really loving Kingsley...he'd cheated on me, too.

I let it go, and fought back tears, and said, "I need to find Hanner."

Kingsley blinked with the sudden shift in conversation. He said, "I was under the impression that she was still gone."

"She's back."

Kingsley had, of course, known about Hanner turning Fang. "I was unaware of that."

"How plugged into this supernatural network are you?" I asked.

"I'm as plugged in as I need to be, or want to be."

"I need to find her," I said. "And Fang."

"I'll see what I can find out," I said.

"They're killing out of L.A." I hesitated to say *training*, although that was what I suspected the killings were.

Kingsley nodded, held my gaze. "Have you considered why they're leaving bodies in the park, Sam?"

"I have."

"Any thoughts?"

"Not many, other than it's obvious they want people to know a vampire is around."

"People?" asked Kingsley. "Or just you?"

"Me?"

"Yes," he said. "You."

"What do you mean?"

"Their actions have flushed you out, in a way."

"But why?"

"I don't know, Sam."

I next told Kingsley about Sanchez's memory gap.

"I think we know the reason for the memory gap, Sam," said Kingsley. "Someone wanted him to contact you."

"But he contacted Sherbet first."

"Which would be protocol, and less obvious," said Kingsley. "Contact Sherbet first, who would obviously turn around and contact you. So, who would know to contact Sherbet first?"

"Hanner," I said.

"And Hanner, according to you, is particularly adept at altering memories."

I looked at Kingsley grimly. "We need to find her, and we need to see what the hell is going on."

Kingsley looked at me with a lot of concern in his big, brown eyes. "And stop the killings, too, right?"

I blinked, realizing I'd overlooked that crucial reasoning. "Yes," I said, mildly alarmed at my oversight, "that, too."

28.

I was seated outside of Detective Rachel Hanner's home in the Fullerton Hills.

It was late and the hills were mostly quiet and I was smoking again. The occasional car drove by, winding up and out of sight, or winding down and out of sight. The homes up here were far too big, and far too beautiful for a lowly private eye. Or even for a homicide detective. Yet, this is where Hanner lived...and lived well.

Detective Sanchez had called me on the way out and asked how the investigation was coming along. I hadn't told Sanchez too much of what I knew. And I certainly hadn't revealed Fang or Hanner's identity. So, I debated about how much to tell him, and finally told him that I was following a very strong lead. He had asked how strong. I said I was going to the vampire's lair. He asked if I really said *lair*, and I said I had and that I would fill him in later.

And lair it was, although it looked less like a lair and more like an opulent home. That a homicide detective lived up here—in the priciest part of Fullerton, no doubt with the attorneys and doctors and Starbucks franchisees, should have been an indicator that something was amiss. Undoubtedly, Hanner had been many things throughout her long life, and had amassed tremendous wealth.

Or not. Who knows. Maybe she had killed the owner of the house and assumed her identity. Truth was, I didn't know much about Hanner.

Yes, we had sat together on her deck, drinking blood. Yes, she had been kind to me early on. She alone had cleaned up two of my messes, back when I had taken on two powerful vampires. One a Texan and the other, perhaps the oldest vampire of all, or one of the oldest. In both cases, witnesses at both scenes had to have their memories cleaned or replaced. Yes, she had been there for me.

As I smoked, hating the taste but enjoying the focus it gave my mind, I knew that it didn't have to be this way with Hanner. She would have been my best friend, if a killing machine like Hanner could have a best friend. I'd never forget the hungry look in her eyes. The feral, wild look of a predator. Yes, she was very far gone. Her humanity often took a backseat to the darkness within.

The *thing* within.

But I had gone against the program, so to speak.

I had bucked the system. As far as I knew, there was not a council of vampires. There was not an official hierarchy or a vampire leader, although I suspected some groups of vampires had banded together here and there. Yes, I thought Hanner was hoping she and I could band together, too, form our own sub-group. I had been on board as far as being her friend, or hanging out with her and learning from her. I had enjoyed our pleasant evenings together...

As a friend, Hanner was creepy at best. As an enemy, she was frightening. I thought she now fell into the latter category.

Now, she was forming a new union with a new vampire.

Fang.

And perhaps setting up another blood ring.

Or worse.

What was worse, I didn't know. But the two of them were up to something. It had been many months since Fang had left with Hanner. I had been given the idea that it was far away, somewhere remote.

But what if it wasn't far away?

What if it had been in my own back yard, so to speak?

What if Hanner and Fang had been in Los Angeles this whole time?

Maybe, I thought, and inhaled deeply on the cancer stick. Then again, they might as well have been a world away if I couldn't find them.

Truth was, I would have let them be.

I would have let them run off together, to be the best goddamn vampires they could be.

That is, if they hadn't left the bodies in Griffith Park.

That is, if they hadn't compelled Detective Sanchez to come calling for Sherbet, and, in turn, me.

They were bringing me into something.

What, exactly, I didn't know.

But I was going to find out.

29.

I snubbed out my cigarette in the minivan's ashtray, reminding myself later to clean it out before the kids got home. Yes, I no longer hid the fact that I was a vampire from my kids, but I still hid the fact that I smoked.

I drummed my fingers on the steering wheel.

It was past midnight, and I felt strong and alert.

Of course, any vampire would be strong and alert. Hanner, for instance, was older than me by many decades, perhaps centuries. A concept that still boggled the mind and, as always, made me seriously question my sanity.

The moon was in its half state. It appeared and disappeared behind the taller trees that ran along this upscale neighborhood. A few cars came by. I was parked behind a bend, between two massive homes. Fullerton Hills might not be Beverly Hills, but these homes were damn nice in my book.

I drummed my fingers some more on the steering wheel, and decided to use what skills I did possess.

I closed my eyes and cast my thoughts out, wondering if I was close enough to Hanner's house to get a good look inside and outside. Turned out I was close enough, although at the far edge of my abilities.

Still, I could see that there were two people inside. A lithe figure who seemed to be moving slowly around the house, and another, broader figure.

Hanner and Fang? No, that wasn't right. Fang was taller than that, and not so broad-shouldered. The woman could have been Hanner, but I wasn't sure. Technically, she was on the run from no one. This was her house. Why shouldn't she be here?

I thought about that.

Hanner had made it personal by going after Fang. Yes, she had fulfilled his wish, but had gone behind my back to do so.

Worse, she was turning my friend into a killer.

Yes, Fang was a big boy, capable of making his own decisions. He had chosen this path. He had wanted to be a vampire from the time his damn canine teeth grew in too long, a fluke of nature that had led to a severe disorder, which led, in turn, to him killing his girlfriend. That murder had made national headlines. His ultimate escape from prison was big news, too. That he was never caught seemed mostly forgotten these days.

I had taken something precious from her—and from many vampires, no doubt. A steady supply of blood.

So, she had taken something from me.

I wasn't a gunslinger, but I knew Hanner and I had a score to settle. It may not go down at high noon in the middle of Main Street, but it was going to go down somewhere, probably at midnight, and probably somewhere a lot more discreet than Main Street.

She knew I had her in my sights. She knew I wanted to take her down, and if I knew Hanner, who was proving to be one hell of a calculating bitch, she was going to come after me first.

I thought about that as I continued drumming my longish, freakish fingernails on the steering wheel.

Finally, I pulled out my cell phone and made a call. Allison picked up on the second ring.

"*Hola*, sweet cheeks," she said. She sounded out of breath.

"What are you doing?"

"Lunges," she said, breathing hard. "I happen to like my own sweet cheeks, thank you very much."

"Are we done talking about our asses?"

"Fine, Grumpy Cat. Where are you? Wait. You're outside a house. A big house. On a hill. I don't know this house."

"Detective Hanner's house," I said.

"Is she back in town?"

"No," I said.

I gave her a peek into my own thoughts. Okay, more than a peek. I gave her access to everything I'd been dealing with for these past few days. And, unlike audible communication, the telepathic kind went quickly. Within a few minutes, she was fully caught up on my situation.

"I agree with you, Sam," said Allison. "I think it's a setup, too."

"Setting me up for what?" I asked.

Allison glugged some water. I could imagine her throwing back her head and drinking intensely. Allison did everything intensely. But, again, I had to use my imagination. Unlike her, my remote viewing only went so far. Allison could see across miles; hell, continents. Me? I could only see a few hundred yards.

"I don't know, Sam," she said when she was done drinking. "But it can't be good. They're willing to kill innocent people to set this trap for you."

"You really think it's a trap?"

"You've been a thorn in Hanner's side for some time now. You could probably turn Fang against her, too. Fang, if I'm understanding you right, seems sort of indebted to her, but I don't understand why he seems so indebted."

I knew what she meant. He seemed unusually loyal.

Allison picked up on my concern. "Can he be compelled by her, Sam?"

"As far as I know, vampires can't control other vampires. I can't read another vampire's mind. Or Kingsley's mind. Or, I suspect, anyone or anything supernatural."

"Either way, Sam, she fears you. You've proven to be stronger than her, and seem to have more powers."

"I've proven to be a bigger freak, you mean."

"No, Sam. That's not what I mean. But think of it this way: she wasn't able to recruit you, so she's probably going to do the next best thing."

I read her mind easily enough. "I thought of that, too," I said.

"Let me help you, Sam."

"No."

"I have powers now. A lot of power. I'm stronger than you know—"

"No," I said, cutting her off. "Out of the question. I'm dealing with Hanner."

"I can help you, Sam—"

"No. End of discussion."

"Why do you get to dictate when the discussion is over?"

"Because I'm the boss. You still work for me, remember?"

It was true. A few months ago, before heading out to the world's creepiest island, I had deputized Allison, so to speak. She was, officially, a private eye in training.

"Fine," she said, throwing a small tantrum. "But you can't just walk into a trap, Sam."

I looked at the dark house before me. "You think the house is a trap?"

"It can't be good, Sam. None of this is good."

"I have to stop her, Allison. And..."

"And bring Fang home?" she said.

"Maybe."

"And what if he doesn't want to come back, Sam? What if he's too far gone?"

I didn't have an answer to that. Instead, I said goodbye and, with her still protesting in my ear, I hung up.

And stepped out of my minivan.

30.

As I approached Hanner's home, I cast my thoughts out again.

More reconnaissance. Yes, there was a woman upstairs, in the kitchen, moving slowly. Almost as if she were drugged. There was a broad-shouldered man sitting at the kitchen table, unmoving.

"Creepy," I whispered.

I was about to return to my body when something told me to keep searching. For what, I did not know, but I'd learned to trust this *something*, this inner guidance system, so to speak.

So, I continued scanning the house, slipping in and out of rooms and hallways and bedrooms. I came across a door and pushed through it, and ended up going down a narrow flight of stairs. The stairs dead-ended into another door, which I mentally pushed through.

Basements were uncommon in California, but not unheard of, especially if someone was a psychopath or a vampire running a secret blood ring. Or both.

The room beyond was small and composed entirely of brick. My guess would be very thick bricks. Sound-proof bricks. There was a drain in the center. Most important, there was a young woman in the room, shackled to the wall, her arms above her head, whimpering uncontrollably. Like something out of a medieval dungeon. She looked like anything but a willing donor.

Jesus.

I snapped back into my body. I considered all my options, from calling Sherbet to breaking the girl out of the basement prison.

In the end, I decided on one course of action.

One obvious course.

I continued up the driveway and up the front steps. There, I gathered myself, and was about to break off the doorknob, when the door opened, and the broad-shouldered man smiled at me.

"Samantha Moon," he said, stepping aside and gesturing toward the interior of the house. "We've been expecting you."

31.

My inner alarm remained silent.

Except this seemed like a damn good time for my inner alarm to be going crazy, but it wasn't. Not a peep. I opened my mouth to speak, to ask who, exactly, had been waiting for me, and who, exactly, he was.

Instead, I studied the man before me. Thick, broad-shouldered, handsome. He wore a frozen smile. Not quite the demonic smile I'd seen recently at the Washington island, but pretty damn close.

"You've been expecting me?" I thought of my conversation with Sanchez. Had she compelled him to report to her, as well? I think probably, which is why he'd called at such a strange time. To follow up. To see where I was in my investigation. And report his findings.

"Yes, Ms. Moon. Won't you please come in? We have some things we need to discuss."

"Some things?"

"Yes."

"What things?"

He smiled even bigger, and now it did look demonic. "Inside, Ms. Moon, if you don't mind."

"And if I do mind?"

He said nothing, only smiled and cocked his head a little, and it occurred to me that he didn't have an answer for that question.

Or, I thought, *he wasn't given an answer.*

I hadn't come across many instances, if any, of another vampire compelling a mortal, but I thought I was seeing one now. Trusting my inner alarm, I nodded and stepped past him. He turned and watched me as I went, and shut the door behind me.

I knew Hanner's home well enough. It was a big home, with the bottom floor dug into the hillside. The upper deck overlooked the rare Orange County woods and the many larger homes beyond, one of which I'd ventured into, meeting, perhaps, the creepiest man on planet earth. A man who had bargained with years from my son's life.

But just as quickly as the old man entered my thoughts, he left again. After all, the smell of blood was thick upon the air.

My stomach growled, and I salivated like the ghoul that I was.

I ignored my stomach, too, and followed the broad-shouldered man through Hanner's home, following a path from the front door to the dining area, a path I had taken a handful of times before this.

The house was dark, except for a single light in the kitchen. Back in the day, back when Hanner and I had been pals, I'd rarely ventured through the house. In fact, she had almost always made it a point to lead me from the kitchen to her balcony with its majestic view of the woodsy canyon.

I hadn't known about the basement.

No, not a basement, I thought, as I followed the man into the kitchen, *a dungeon—a torture dungeon.*

I shuddered. And as I did so, I saw three figures waiting for me in the kitchen. Two were living, and one was very much dead.

The living figure was the woman I had seen in my surveillance of the house. She was sitting alone at the far end of a long dining room table. Before her was a cloth napkin. There was something clearly under the napkin, something small and lumpy. The cloth napkin was stained crimson. The woman, who was maybe in her early thirties, was smiling, too. That same serene and creepy smile.

The ghost behind her was of a woman, but decidedly younger, perhaps in her early twenties. The ghost was particularly bright and well-defined, which meant she'd died recently. At least, that was what my experience told me. Anyway, her ethereal, energetic body crackled with living shards of light, light so bright that I was stunned these two couldn't see her. Then again, maybe they could and were ignoring her, but I doubted it. I had only to remember my pre-freak days, back when I couldn't see such spirits, either. Those were good days.

It was obvious that her neck had been cut open with something sharp. Her static body was so well-defined that I could actually see ghostly hints of tendons and muscle inside of her exposed neck. Whoever she was, she'd been drained and killed, right here in Hanner's house.

The man, oblivious to the spirit, went over and stood by the side of the seated woman. They both smiled at me, both cocking their heads, both compelled to act against their wills.

"How do you two know Detective Hanner?" I asked them.

The man spoke. "We are her private source." He sounded excited, like this was an honor, a privilege, and something as great as being chosen for the next manned mission to the moon.

"You live here?" I asked.

"Yes," he answered, sounding, if possible, even more excited. "We both do."

I noticed their wedding rings. "Are you two married?"

"Yes," said the woman. As she spoke, she kept her head tilted to the side. "We met Detective Hanner on our honeymoon."

"How long ago?"

The man and woman continued staring at me, continued smiling and tilting their heads. "Over three years now," said the man.

"You've lived here for three years?"

They both looked at me, blinked, and smiled. "Oh, yes," they said in unison.

I shook my head and took in some air and continued smelling the strong scent of the red stuff. Blood, that is. Everywhere. In particular, something bloody under the napkin before the woman.

Hanner had met the young couple. Compelled them to follow her home while they had been on their honeymoon, no less. Probably the couple had met a certain specification for Hanner. I suspected they neither had family nor many friends. Few would look for them. And those who did would easily be turned away by a simple phone call that would reassure anyone concerned that they were okay. Hanner, in effect, had kidnapped them.

"Who's in the basement?" I asked.

"A bleeder," said the man.

"A bleeder?"

"Yes."

"What's a bleeder?"

"We bleed her for others, Samantha Moon. In fact, we have recently bled her for you. Would you care for a drink? It's chilling in the refrigerator now."

I should have shuddered. I should have recoiled in horror. I should have called Sherbet to come out and shut this craziness down.

Instead, I found myself about to nod. My ears rang a bit. And my thoughts were fuzzy.

In fact, I started to nod, then shook my head vigorously. As I did so, I backed up—but not at the reality of an innocent woman who was being bled in the basement below. But at the horror of my very, very strong bloodlust.

Yesss, came a single word from the depths of my mind. *Yesss, yesss, yesss, yesss....*

Fresh blood. Procured unwillingly. Taken against another's will was *her* ultimate craving. Such blood, I knew, would feed not me...but *her.*

"No," I heard myself say, as the hissing continued, a long, slow leak just inside my eardrum. "No, thank you."

"Are you sure, Samantha Moon? It was tapped for you and you alone. It will be wasted otherwise."

Well, in that case... I wanted to say, but I didn't.

Tapped, he had said. Like tapping a maple tree. This should have sounded horrific to me. But it didn't. No, it sounded intriguing. It sounded... interesting. *Tell me more about this tapping business*, I wanted to say.

But I didn't.

I rubbed my head, pressed my fingers hard into my temples. She was in here somewhere. Where she was, exactly, I didn't know. But she was getting bolder, stronger.

No...she was getting desperate.

She wants out.

She wants her freedom.

Her freedom meant my imprisonment, of course.

I took in a lot of air and held it and willed her out of my mind, and the hissing, finally, faded

165

slowly away. I expelled the air and looked at the compelled couple.

"No, thank you," I said again.

Behind them, the ghost faded in and out of existence. Once or twice, she looked at me, but she was lost. Lost even before death, I suspected. A runaway, I sensed. Lost and forgotten, even in life and death. How many other such spirits were here, I didn't know, but I suspected more.

"Why don't you go home?" I said to the couple.

"We are home, Samantha Moon," said the woman.

"We are *very* happy here," said the man.

I doubted that. I doubted they even knew what they were saying. I suspected that Hanner's compulsion was so extensive that she controlled them either from afar, or gave them pre-recorded responses, so to speak.

"Why were you waiting for me?" I asked.

"Because our mistress said you would come."

I looked at them again. Had they been recently fed upon? Hard to know, since vampire wounds inflicted on mortals—those living, that is—healed almost instantly, as was my experience with Allison. But I was suddenly sure of one thing.

"She was here recently," I said.

They said nothing.

"Tell me, goddammit."

They continued smiling, heads tilted to one side. They both blinked together.

From below, I heard the chained woman crying

up through the floorboards. The bleeder, as they had called her. Bleeders, I suspected, didn't last long in the house of horrors.

When Hanner had been here, I didn't know, and how she knew I would come calling, I didn't know that either.

No, I thought. She would have known. Everything she had done, thus far, had been orchestrated to lead me here. But why?

I looked again at the bloody tissue before them.

"What's under the napkin?" I asked, although I suddenly didn't want to know.

The woman nodded slightly and straightened her head for the first time. She rested the flat of her palms on the table. She held my gaze. "Mistress has a message for you, Samantha Moon."

I swallowed and stepped forward. Curious and repulsed at the same time, horrified yet intrigued.

What's wrong with me? I thought.

"Mistress wanted you to see this."

And with that, the woman lifted the napkin. Underneath was a severed finger...a pinkie finger with a ring still attached to it. I knew the ring. It was Danny's pimp ring, as I called it. An ugly garnet ring, too big for any man to wear with a straight face. He loved that ring.

Had I any color in my face, I suspected it would have drained about now.

"What the hell did she do with Danny?"

"We don't know," said the man. "But he is the first."

"The first what, goddammit?"

The finger had been neatly severed, with the use of a knife, no doubt. Blood crusted around the open end. I could see the dozens of dark hairs lying flat across one side, beneath the main knuckle.

"Master wanted you to know that she will systematically kill your entire family until you meet her."

"I'm here now," I said, unable to take my eyes off the pale finger. *Oh, Jesus, Danny...*

"Not here, Samantha Moon."

"Then where?"

"She will tell you."

"Where is she?"

"Mistress is busy at the moment."

I nearly leaped across the table. Nearly strangled them both. But I couldn't. They were just the messengers, after all.

For the first time in a long time, I felt sick to my stomach. "Busy doing what?"

They both looked at me for a heartbeat or two, and for the briefest of moments, I sensed a small wave of compassion coming from them. But then, that compassion was gone as quickly as it had appeared.

"She is seeking another."

"Another *what*, goddammit?"

But they didn't answer. They only smiled and looked at me and stood together at the far end of the table, heads cocked to one side. As if listening to someone or something I couldn't hear.

32.

I was back in my minivan.

Had my body been any less than it was, I would have been hyperventilating. My hands were shaking as I did my best to dial my sister's home number without crushing the phone into pieces.

Now I waited in the dark while the phone rang, the light of the half-moon above coming through the big windshield.

"C'mon," I said. "c'mon."

Mercifully, thankfully, the call was answered after three rings. It was Rick, Mary Lou's husband, a man, I suspected, who knew my secret, although Mary Lou claimed to have never told him.

"Hi, Sam," he said pleasantly enough, although I always detected a hint of reservation in his voice.

"Hi, Ricky," I said, forcing myself to stay calm. "Can I speak to Mary Lou?"

"She went out to get some tacos. You can try her cell."

I said I would and then asked, as calmly as I could, about my kids.

"They're here, playing something called 'Go, Go, Racer Go.' Damn game nearly gave me an epileptic seizure."

I'd been holding my breath after my question, and expelled it now, perhaps a little too loudly.

"Is everything okay, Sam?"

"Yes."

He paused. "Are you sure?"

"Yes," I said. "I'm going to try Mary Lou now."

"Good, and ask her where the hell she is." He laughed lightly. "She left an hour ago."

I nearly hung up on him. I said I would and was soon dialing her number in such a rush that I screwed it up twice, dialing Kingsley both times by mistake. I hung up on him both times.

I got it right on my third attempt and it rang once.

"Hello, Samantha," said a familiar and cold voice. A female voice that instantly shot dread through me.

The voice, of course, belonged to Hanner.

33.

"Where's my sister?"

"She's here, Samantha."

"If you've hurt her—"

"I have not hurt her, Sam. Not yet. Now, Danny on the other hand, is a different story. Speaking of hands..."

"What have you done with him?"

"I remembered your stories, Sam. I remembered how he hurt you and cheated on you and tried to destroy you. Danny is fair game."

My stomach dropped. Danny was a bastard...but he didn't deserve this. He was the father of my kids. A worthless father, yes, but their father, nonetheless.

"Is he dead?" I asked.

"Not yet, Samantha. But he will be. Along with your sister." She paused ever so slightly. "And you, too, of course."

I detected a strange note in her voice. Her answers were monotone, automatic. I also detected a slight hiss. "I'm not speaking to Detective Hanner, am I?"

"You are perceptive, Sssamantha Moon." The hiss was stronger now, more pronounced.

"If you kill me," I said, "then you kill *her*, too."

I was, of course, referring to the demon within me.

"Not quite, Sssamantha. Our sssister has decided that you are too problematic, too difficult. She wishes to move into a new host. We have the perfect host with us. She looks remarkably like you, Sssamantha. But, we suspect, she will be much more manageable."

I ran my fingers through my thick hair. "I must die for her to leave me?"

"You are a fassst learner, Missss Moon."

"Who are you, godammit? Why are you doing this?"

"Yes, we are damned, very damned. Which is exactly *why* we are doing this."

"What do you want with me?" I asked.

"We want you to die, Samantha Moon. And our host, here, your one-time friend Detective Hanner, is just the one to do it."

"What have you done with my sister?"

"She's here with us, Sam. Sitting quietly in the front seat like a good girl. Like a good future host. We suspect she will be much, much more manageable."

"If you fucking touch her..."

"We will do much more than touch her, Samantha. But first, of course, you must die."

I took in a lot of air. I couldn't get a read on Hanner, as she was immortal. And I couldn't get a read on my sister, either, as she was my blood relative. Dammit. I couldn't even get a read on Danny, as he and I had never connected deeply enough to develop that bond, which told me a lot about my ex-husband.

"What do you want me to do?" I asked.

"We want you to meet us, Sssamantha. We have a good place in mind for you to die."

Then, the demon told me where to go, although this time she sounded very much like Hanner.

And then the line went dead.

34.

I was at Allison's apartment in Beverly Hills.

It was all I could do not to call Kingsley again. In fact, I had nearly done so as I drove to Allison's house in a blind rush. Yes, I nearly flew there, too. But the truth was, I wanted the hour drive from Orange County to Beverly Hills to think this through. And I knew I needed the van to bring Mary Lou home and take Danny to…a hospital.

That drive hadn't helped much.

The thinking soon turned to panic, and I didn't accomplish anything other than nearly killing a half dozen other drivers as I whipped around them recklessly, aiming my screaming minivan to Beverly Hills, and to Allison's place.

Now she was sitting at a table with a rolled-up napkin in front of her. A rolled-up napkin with bloodstains. Allison looked sick. She should have looked sick. There was, after all, a severed finger in front of her.

"This can't be happening, Sam."

I was pacing in front of her. I was alternately wringing my hands and shaking them, trying to come to terms with the fact that a rogue vampire possessed by a hellish demon currently had my sister...and Danny.

Danny. How the devil had *he* gotten in on this?

I didn't know, but I had his finger and ring in a rolled-up napkin to prove it. And I'd had Hanner answering my sister's cell phone to prove she had Mary Lou, too.

"Yes," I said to Allison, who had, undoubtedly, been following my hectic train of thought. "This is happening."

"But I don't understand, Sam. Why drag you out to...where is it? I'm seeing a tunnel system in your thoughts?"

"It's a cavern," I said, "beneath the Los Angeles River."

"Where's that?"

"Not far from here," I said. I had to Google Map it, too, being an Orange County girl myself. "It flows between Griffith Park and Glendale."

"You mean that big ditch."

"That big ditch was once a natural river, and had only within the past seventy-five years been controlled and cemented."

"And did you say *beneath* the river?"

"Yes."

"What, exactly, is beneath the river?"

"An old cave network and something that, I think, is a cavern, from the way Hanner described it."

"A cavern? Under the river?"

"Under it or close to it, which is why I need you now."

Allison, who was tuned into my mind and following my thoughts almost as fast as I could think them, said, "Oh, gross."

"It's the only way, Allison. I can't lock onto my sister or Fang or even Danny. And even if I could, my range only goes so far."

Her range was, of course, potentially global. In fact, there didn't seem to be any limit to Allison's ability to see distantly. Remote viewing, as it was called in psychic circles.

Earlier, after getting directions to the underground caverns beneath the Los Angeles River, I'd dashed back in the house, where I had found the newlyweds sitting and standing in the same position I had left them in, and snatched the finger and the napkin.

Now, it was sitting in front of Allison, who'd been staring down at it for the past ten minutes.

"Please, Allison. I need your help."

The color had drained from her face instantly when she's caught on what was inside the napkin. She'd been pale ever since. I was fairly certain she'd yet to look away from the wrapped package sitting before her. Finally, she nodded. "He went through a lot of pain, Sam."

"I can imagine."

"But..." she trailed off, but I caught her psychic hit just as it occurred to her.

"Jesus," I said.

"Yes, Sam. He's involved with this somehow. Entangled. Not completely innocent."

I shook my head and swore and cursed my ex-husband all over again. My stupid, stupid ex-husband. So stupid that he had lost a finger.

"He was trying to exact revenge," said Allison.

"Did you just say *exact revenge*?"

"Yes. I know it sounds cheesy, but that's the feeling I get. He was trying to get back at you, somehow. To stop you somehow. To control you somehow."

"And he teamed up with Hanner."

"Or she teamed up with him," said Allison.

"He made a deal with the devil," I said. "Literally."

Allison nodded and we both looked down at the wrapped finger. Yes, Danny had paid a heavy price for his stupidity—and his hate for me, but I didn't have time to think about that now. I had to see what I was up against. I had to see—through Allison's remote viewing—what the hell was going on.

"It's time, Allison," I said.

We both knew what that meant. She nodded, then slowly reached forward and began unrolling the greasy napkin. As she did so, she calmly got up, walked over to the nearby bathroom, and wretched for a half minute. She came back, wiping her mouth, gave me a weak smile, and then sat before the still-rolled up napkin.

She undid it completely...and, after taking a deep breath and visibly fighting the rising vomit at the back of her throat, took hold of the severed finger in both her hands.

35.

"I see him," said Allison.

I saw him, too, but I waited for her to make sense of what she was seeing, for her to focus, to hone in, to get a feel for the place. To, quite literally, slip inside.

More details came through.

In her thoughts, I saw Danny in a chair. No, a desk. Perhaps a high school desk, as he seemed to fit in it well enough. Both arms were lying across the flat surface of the desk. Both arms were secured with duct tape. Both hands hung over the lip of the desk. Blood dripped steadily from the gaping maw where his right pinkie had been. The wound itself looked badly infected...and old. How long Danny had been down there, I didn't know. I realized I hadn't heard from him in about a week. Nothing unusual about that. He saw the kids every other week. And sometimes, he even missed those dates. I'd gone as long as two or three weeks without hearing from the sleazy bastard.

Danny looked like hell, and my heart went out to him, despite everything. I forgot that he had turned on me...and that his current situation was, apparently, a direct result of him trying to hurt me.

As I watched him sobbing and shaking, I saw the chains around his bare ankles. The skin was bloody and raw and mostly peeled away. Dried blood pooled around his bare feet. For once, in a long time, the sight of blood did not trigger a hunger in me. The sight of Danny and his wounds, instead, triggered a deep sadness...

And anger.

Although I could see what Allison could see, she got a far better picture than I ever could: "I see a big room. Rock walls. Yes, a cavern. It appears natural, although some of it could have been chiseled. Danny is in the room, crying softly to himself. I can feel his fear, his pain, his self-hatred. He hates that he put himself into this mess, hates you even more for introducing him to this dark world. A part of him, a very small part of him, understands that this wasn't your fault, that your attack seven years ago was unprovoked, that you, in fact, never asked for this. That small part of him is overshadowed by his fear and hatred for you, Sam. He feels abandoned and humiliated and angry."

"Is he alone?" I asked.

"Hold on..."

And now, Allison's perspective widened further as she searched the room. She might as well have been an actual bat, swooping around the room. Her remote viewing ability was uncanny. Then again, I didn't know much about any of this. Maybe her abilities were normal for one who allowed a vampire to feed from her. Maybe the newlyweds in Hanner's home had such abilities, too.

Or not. I knew Allison had started out as psychic, and that my feeding upon her only made her more psychic. And, of course, she had been a witch down through the ages. And so had I.

But not in this life. No. And if my immortality held up, perhaps never again.

As Allison swooped mentally through the room, I followed her thoughts as best as I could, her path, as if I was swooping right there with her. It was thrilling and bizarre, but I didn't think much of any of that. This was, after all, a recon mission. Meaning, we were here to gather information—anything that would help me save Mary Lou and, yes, Danny, and help get us all out alive.

"There," I said. I directed her thoughts toward a dark opening in the far wall.

Allison oriented on that and we swooped down through the cavern and into the opening and into yet another cavern, this one smaller, and this one occupied by more people.

I saw them through Allison's perception. Unfortunately, this cavern was mostly dark...and Allison could not see through the dark. Or, perhaps, her distance sight could not see through the dark. But there were a few torches on the wall, and enough to see a handful of people I didn't recognize.

The cavern, I saw, was something out of *The Lost Boys*...filled with old and new furniture, haphazardly arranged, tapestries and paintings on the walls, statues and trinkets. Most of it looked old, and some of it even looked valuable. Mostly, the room looked like a big hangout.

"It's a sort of safe house," said Allison. I knew she could read deeper into what she was seeing than I could; feel deeper, too. "It's where vampires go when on the run, or when they are new."

"A training facility," I said.

"Something like that. But it's also more. There are old vampires who dominate here. Powerful vampires. They kill here, too. They plot and plan and kill and train."

"A sort of supernatural headquarters," I said.

"Yes," said Allison faintly. She was scanning the room, searching for what we had yet to find.

"Can you hear anything?" I asked.

Allison shook her head. "I can only see...and feel."

"Do you see my sister?"

"Not yet, Sam."

I was still seeing what Allison saw, as she swooped through the room. "Can they see you?" I asked.

I sensed Allison almost smile...then again, it

was hard to smile when you were holding a severed finger. "No, Sam. They are unaware of our snooping."

"You're a good sidekick to have around," I said.

"Partner," she said.

"We'll see," I said.

"There!" said Allison suddenly. I saw it, too. Three figures emerged into the room. Detective Hanner, my sister and Fang.

My sister was blindfolded, and plastic ties held her hands together. She was sobbing and stumbling as Hanner pulled her along.

They were met by someone I had seen before.

Someone I had fought before.

Someone—or something—that had nearly killed me, if not for Kingsley's help.

It was, quite possibly, the oldest vampire in the world. The same vampire who had kidnapped a boy he had thought was my son, a vampire I had fought under the Mission Inn Dome.

It was Dominique.

"Okay," I said, reaching out and touching Allison's arm. "I've seen enough."

36.

I was pacing.

The finger was back in the napkin and on ice in Allison's freezer, although she didn't seem too thrilled about that.

"Because there's a severed finger with my green peas, Sam. You wouldn't be too thrilled either," she said defensively.

But I wasn't paying her much attention. My thoughts were focused on the caverns beneath the Los Angeles River. Most importantly, on how to get my sister and my rat bastard of an ex-husband out alive.

"And Fang," said Allison suddenly.

I paused and looked at her. "What?"

"It's there in your thoughts, Sam, although you haven't acknowledged it. You also want to get Fang out. To save him."

"I..." But I didn't know what to say. So, I closed my mouth.

"He's one of them, Sam. A kidnapper and a killer."

I didn't know what to say to that, either, except that I didn't share Allison's convictions. I knew Fang, perhaps better than anyone. He was not a psychopathic killer.

As I thought those words, I picked up Allison's thought: *Once a killer, Sam, always a killer.*

I shook my head and ran my hands through my hair and thought about what I had to do. They took my sister. They took my ex-husband. *My God, they cut off his finger.* They were going to kill him, I was sure of it. They were going to kill me, too. The evil bitch inside me was getting impatient, growing weary of my resistance. Well, fuck her. And fuck them, too.

Poor Mary Lou. She hadn't asked for any of this. She had been heading out to get, what, tacos for the family? And that piece of shit Hanner had been waiting for her? Waiting because Sanchez had reported my activities to her. Sanchez was a good cop who had been compelled to do a traitorous thing. My guess was that he wouldn't remember calling her.

"It's a trap, Samantha," said Allison. "It's been a trap all along."

I didn't say anything, but kept pacing. I knew that, of course.

"Sam, when I was in those caverns, I sensed

something else, something that I think you might not have picked up on, something that occurred when Fang, Hanner and your sister appeared."

I stopped in front of my friend, who, only now, was getting some of the color back to her cheeks since dealing with the finger. "What?" I asked.

"They're getting rid of you for another reason."

"What reason?"

She swallowed, looked at me. "I mean, they are going to *try* to get rid of you."

"I know what you meant, dammit. What's the other reason?"

"It's Fang," she said. "They sense great potential in him. Great potential to kill. I felt it from Hanner and the other vampire."

"You can read other vampires?"

"Only immortals can't read each other, Sam. I'm not immortal and I'm growing stronger, thanks to you."

"You're doing a lot more than remote viewing," I pointed out.

"I think of it as remote sensing." She shrugged. "It's a growing ability."

Like me, Allison's abilities seemed to be progressing rapidly. Unlike me, her abilities were tied to my drinking of her blood.

"Not just blood," she corrected. "Blood isn't the only source of my power. I'm developing my abilities in other ways now."

"Witchcraft," I said.

"Of course," she said.

"Fine," I said. "What about the other vampires? What else is going on?"

"Like I said, Sam. They sense great potential in him."

"Potential to do what?"

"To kill, to supply and perhaps someday to lead. Mostly, they sense in him a willingness to go along with the program."

"To give himself up to them," I said. Or, put another way, to allow himself to be controlled, possessed and perhaps taken over by the evil within him, too.

"Yes, Sam, except for one problem, which is where you come in."

I stopped pacing and stood before her. I was surprised to discover that my heart had suddenly started beating faster than normal. Hell, faster than it had in some time.

"What are you getting at?" I asked.

"His love for you," said Allison. "It's posing a problem, a hindrance."

My heart continued pounding, and knowing that Fang still felt something for me—anything for me —was a gift I wasn't entirely prepared for. I would have felt excitement—and hope—if not for the fact that he and the others had my sister.

"They need you dead, Sam, so that they can properly cultivate him for greater things."

"I have to leave," I said, grabbing my keys and opening the front door.

"I'm coming with you."

"No, you're not."

"Sam, you need me."

"No, I don't—"

I hadn't quite finished my sentence when the front door suddenly slammed shut again. I jumped, startled. I was about to ask what the holy hell had happened when I turned and saw Allison holding out her right hand, her eyelids half closed.

"Jesus. Was that you?" I asked.

"Like I told you, Sam, my powers are growing." She lowered her hand and opened her eyes.

"Well, it's a nice trick, dear," I said, opening the door again, "but I'm still not bringing—"

She turned, raising her hand. The comfy over-stuffed chair and a half, where I had sat many times before, lifted off the floor and hurled through the apartment. Pillows and Allison's purse, which had all been on the chair, went flying in different directions. Unfortunately, the chair was heading for the sliding glass door, which led to her patio and a nice third-story view of the other Beverly Hills apartments. I braced for the coming crash when the chair—sweet Jesus—stopped in mid-air. Stopped just before the glass door. The chair rotated slowly...and settled carefully onto the floor.

"Holy hell," I said.

"Now, can I come with you, Sam?" she asked, opening her eyes and lowering her arm.

"Sweet mama," I said.

"I second that," said a deep voice behind me. A voice I recognized.

I turned to find Kingsley standing in the doorway, filling it completely, wearing jeans and a black tee shirt and hair down to his shoulders. Good cologne wafted from him as if the stuff flowed from his veins.

Allison said, "Oh, did I forget to mention that I called Kingsley, too?"

37.

We were in my minivan.

It wasn't exactly the Batmobile, or something cooked up by *Iron Man*'s Richard Stark. It was just an older minivan—the same minivan I used to pick my kids up from school, to buy groceries and to run errands. Just last week, I'd backed into a pole at my kids' school, putting a good-sized dent in the bumper that was going to cost me more money to fix than I wanted to spend.

And here we were, charging through the night. Three freaks to battle a cavern full of freaks.

Yeah, my life is weird.

"You shouldn't have called him," I said to Allison for the tenth time.

"Hey," said Kingsley, "you say that enough times and I might start getting offended."

"Well, she shouldn't have called you."

"Yeah, you mentioned that. Except I'm not going to let you walk alone into a vampire nest."

"Is that a politically correct thing to say?" asked Allison from the backseat.

"You keep quiet," I said to her, aiming the minivan down Sunset Boulevard. I kept the car at well over the speed limit, not giving a damn about a ticket. Hell, I would compel the fucking cop to forget what he saw and to crave a pink donut instead.

And, yes, I thought of Sherbet, and, yes, I wished he was here, too. Same with my other detective friends: Knighthorse, Spinoza and Aaron King, who may or may not be Elvis.

No, I thought, shaking my head again. *I can't put them—or anyone—in jeopardy.*

"You also can't do this alone," said Allison, reading my mind.

"Huh?" said Kingsley. "Oh, I see. You two are doing your mind-reading thing."

I was fairly certain the minivan was listing to his side. I swear to God, Kingsley was bigger than the last time I'd seen him. Kingsley would, in fact, keep growing, minutely, with each transformation.

So weird, I thought.

Earlier, I'd made a number of my own calls. First up, I had called Mary Lou's husband. I had told him I was with Mary Lou and something important had come up that we couldn't talk about. I suggested very strongly that he should stay indoors and make dinner there. He agreed. A little too quickly.

Yes, I had used some of my own compulsion on him. No, I didn't have any clue that it would actually go through the call. But it had.

Next, I called both Anthony and Tammy in turn. Yes, they each had their own cell phones. And, yes, they each cost me an arm and a leg. But, dammit, I loved knowing I could get a hold of my kids at any time of the day. And, yes, they had strict orders to keep their cell phones with them at all times—and on. Anyway, I told them each to watch out for each other. Tammy, my telepathic daughter—yes, a family of freaks—picked up a stray thought of mine that her aunt was in trouble. I told her to keep that information to herself and that I was doing all I could to help her aunt.

Finally, as I had been heading out to Allison's, I called Sherbet—and kept my mind closed in the process. I hadn't wanted him to know where we were, or what we were up to. But I had asked him to keep an eye on my sister's house. He had told me he would do it himself, with one of his officers. He had asked if everything was okay. I had told him no, everything was *not* okay. He said he wanted to help, and I had told him no. He didn't like it and insisted and I told him no again. He still didn't like it, but finally gave in, and told me to stay safe. I told him I would do my best, and, before we hung up, I told him to send a car out to Hanner's. He asked why and I told him he wouldn't believe me if I told him. He said try him, so I do, telling him about the newlyweds and the bleeder. Sherbet then said that I was right, he didn't believe me, but he would send someone out right away.

As I drove, Allison caught Kingsley up on the layout of the caverns, as she had seen them remotely.

Kingsley shook his shaggy, blockish head. "Your powers have grown considerably since the last time I saw you."

Which had, of course, been at Skull Island months, ago. Back then, Allison was just coming into her own, just exploring her increased powers.

"You could say I've had an epiphany," she said from the backseat, sticking her head between us.

"What kind of epiphany?" he asked.

"I'm a witch."

Kingsley glanced down at her, somehow managing to see through all his thick hair. "Witches scare the shit out of me."

That was news to me. Truth was, I didn't think anything scared the big oaf. "Why?" I asked.

"They're unpredictable...and seem to have nature on their side. And after the demonstration I just saw at your house...well, remind me to stay on your good side."

Allison beamed, but as she did so, I sensed her self-doubt. Yes, this was all new to her. Yes, she could perform some incredible tricks, but, no, she did not feel worthy of her newfound—and growing —powers.

Truth was, I didn't know much about any of this

stuff, either, let alone what a witch could and couldn't do.

Not true, Samantha, came Allison's thought, as she picked up on my own. *You were once a witch, too. We both were.*

Along with Millicent, I added, referring to the spirit that had first broken the news to Allison of her supernatural pedigree.

Yes, Millicent. And we were both supposed to be witches again, except you've taken a slightly different path.

A bloodsucking path, I thought grimly.

Well, we're together again, said Allison, *and that's all that matters.*

"Are you two quite done?" asked Kingsley.

"What do you mean?" I asked.

"Your telepathy crap...it's kind of rude."

"How did you know we were doing telepathy?" I asked, genuinely intrigued.

"Because the two of you get all quiet at the exact same time, which is rare enough as it is. Were you two talking about me?"

"Maybe," I said, and, despite the seriousness of our current situation, and despite knowing my sister was at the hands of forces that would love nothing more than to rip her life away from her, I giggled. So did Allison.

"C'mon. What were you two talking about?"

"Your hair," said Allison, lying and giggling some more.

"What about my hair?" asked Kingsley defensively. For some reason, the big gorilla was always defensive about his thick locks.

"We think you need a haircut," said Allison.

"We do?" I asked her.

"Yes, we do," she said.

"Okay," I said, laughing some more. "We do."

"Well, I can't cut it," said Kingsley.

This was news to me. Despite having dated the big goof for a while, I hadn't known this fact.

"Why not?" we both asked at once.

"It just grows right back, within days, and sometimes within hours. And, even worse, it always grows back a little longer."

I think Kingsley was trying to get our sympathy, but he got the exact opposite reaction. Allison and I burst out laughing. I wasn't expecting to laugh. I was pissed and ready to take on every fucking vampire in Los Angeles if I had to. But now, I found myself laughing, nearly uncontrollably. The van swerved. Kingsley gripped the dashboard, and I laughed even harder. Truth was, I think I needed to laugh. And hearing Allison's snorting in the backseat made me totally lose it.

"Are you two quite done?" growled Kingsley, shaking his head.

"When he cuts his hair," said Allison, sitting forward between us, gasping and wiping her eyes, her voice barely above a squeak, "it just keep growing out even longer...within days...hours... that's the funniest thing I've ever heard."

I wasn't sure if it was the funniest thing I'd ever

heard, but it was definitely a tension breaker for me. And as I gasped and fought for my own breath, Kingsley mumbled, "I don't know why I open up to you two."

"And now we know why you don't ask for a free haircut, either," squealed Allison.

I reached back and put a hand on my friend's forearm. "Let's leave him alone," I said. "We don't want to piss him—or his hair—off."

Allison giggled some more, while Kingsley shot me a grumpy look. "It's really not funny," he said.

"No," I said, struggling to keep a straight face. "Excessive hair growth is never funny."

Allison literally snorted in the back seat, which made Kingsley finally crack a smile. "You two are clowns," he said. "I think we should get serious."

"Yes, serious," Allison and I said together. We stopped laughing almost on cue, even though Allison might have snorted once more for good measure.

I turned left from Sunset and headed up Los Feliz Boulevard, following my recently added navigational device. No, this old van did not come with navigation, but this one worked easily enough...that is, if it would quit falling from its mount, which it did now as I made my left turn. I caught it and returned it to its spot before I had completed the turn.

"If you two are done making fun of my affliction, maybe we should discuss a game plan."

I turned left into one of the Griffith Park

entrances, stopped the van and killed the engine.

"Good idea," I said. "Oh, and we're here."

38.

We sat in the minivan.

Technically, the park was closed, but there was nothing to keep us out either. The park was, after all, an entire hillside...a chain of hillsides, in fact.

"She told me to come alone," I said.

"And what did you say?" asked Kingsley.

"I told her to go fuck herself."

"That's my girl," said Kingsley. "So, where is this place?"

"The river—which is now an aqueduct—flows not too far from here. It's popular with bikers and joggers."

"And vampires," said Allison.

"And how do we get to their underground lair?" asked Kingsley

I nearly asked the big guy to quit calling it a *lair*, except that's exactly what it was. A breeding ground for the undead. A nest, perhaps.

"There's a cave opening close to here," I said. "She described it to me."

In fact, as I spoke those words, I told the gang to hold on while I closed my eyes and cast my thoughts out. Unlike Allison, who needed something personal, I needed no such aid. At any point, in any place, I could close my eyes and cast my mind out, scanning my immediate surroundings within a few hundred feet. And, yes, that net seemed to be growing wider these days, but not by much. Still a couple of hundred feet, give or take.

My sweeping, all-seeing internal eye didn't have any problems with the dark either. The night was bright and alive and I could have just as easily been a dark demigod looking down at his realm.

Or the world's weirdest mom trying to save her sister.

Either way, I confirmed that the park was empty of anything human. It was also empty of most things animal, except for a few stray cats and a squirrel that seemed to be dancing the jig on a nearby tree branch. I next searched for the landmark Hanner had described: a red post off to the side of the main river path. *There, found it.* Next, I mentally hung a left and continued on to a pile of boulders—and found them exactly where Hanner had said they would be. I also found the small opening into the rocks—an opening that might pose a problem for Kingsley, and slipped inside it, but not very far. I had reached the limits of my abilities.

One thing was certain, though, the cave entrance was not guarded.

A moment later, I returned to my body, waited a moment to get reoriented, and then reported my findings. Mostly, I reported them for Kingsley's benefit, as I knew Allison had internally followed my traveling, swooping mind.

"I'll fit," said Kingsley.

"How can you be so sure?"

He tapped his thick skull. "Mind over matter."

"Fine," I said, "so what's the game plan?"

"Get your sister," said Kingsley, "and get the hell out of there."

"What about Danny?" I asked.

Kingsley turned and looked at me, and as he did so, his eyes flared amber. Not the flame I sometimes saw in other vampires' eyes. No, this was the glint of something wild, feral, untamed. Something animalistic.

"Well, I can't just leave him there," I said.

"He's part of this, Sam. You told me so yourself. That they turned on him is his own fault."

"He's my kids' father..."

"He made his own bed, Samantha," said Kingsley.

As he said those words, I wondered about that. I wondered if Danny had, indeed, made his bed, or if someone had made it for him, so to speak. Well, I would learn the truth soon enough. One thing was certain, there was no way in hell he had willingly allowed his finger to be cut off.

I didn't mention Fang, although Allison was well aware of my plans to save him, too. Kingsley already didn't like Fang much, and vice versa. Both saw the other as a threat, and if Kingsley was already having a problem with me helping my ex, well, I knew for damn sure he would put his overgrown paw down in regard to Fang.

He doesn't like Fang, came Allison's thoughts.

You can read his mind, too? I asked, surprised.

Not really. Kingsley is a master at shielding his thoughts, but I can read his body language and some latent feelings he's had. If you are going to save Fang, and possibly even your ex, you can count him out.

And what about you? I asked her.

Oh, you can always count me in, silly.

Fang has the diamond medallion, I thought, referring to the one artifact that could return me to a mostly-normal life.

I know, Sam. Is that the only reason why you want to save him?

I didn't have to think long about the answer. *No,* I thought back to her, *I'm pretty sure I love him.*

That's what I thought, Sam.

"Are you two done?" asked Kingsley.

"We're done," I said.

"Good," he said, "because I have an idea about how we can save your sister...and maybe even your lying, cheating ex-hubby, too."

39.

The trail from the parking lot soon wound along the Los Angeles River.

No, not a traditional river, but it had been once, before man, concrete and zoning commissions debased, muzzled and graffitied it. As we followed a dirt path that led along the flowing water, which sparkled to my eyes, but probably not so much to Allison's—Kingsley was a different story—I scanned ahead, verifying that we were not being followed or stepping into a trap. We were okay on both fronts.

So far.

Crickets chirped endlessly, seemingly coming from everywhere at once. A small hum filled the air, too; mosquitoes were alive and well along the banks of the tamed river. Beyond, the drone of traffic along the I-5. Many people didn't realize just how hilly Los Angeles was. We were surrounded by such hills now, each dotted with bright lights from bigger homes.

A friend of mine, Spinoza, had his office near here, in Echo Park. So did another friend of mine, who bore an uncanny resemblance to Elvis Presley, despite the obvious facial reconstruction.

We probably could have used both their help now. But they were mortals with guns. These were vampires with teeth. Vamps with teeth trumped guns.

I had another friend out here, too, a private eye who had recently passed from lung cancer complicated by AIDS. I'd met him long ago while working with the federal government. We'd both been involved with a missing girl case, a case on which many government agencies and local police and private eyes had found themselves working. We never did find the girl, but I had met James Coleman. His good friend, a stoic Nigerian named Numi, had been kind enough to send me an email about his passing. I would miss James. He had been a troubled guy, but a great investigator.

I took my thoughts off James and put them onto my poor sister, who didn't deserve any of this. God, she was going to be so pissed off at me. And, yes, I was already assuming that we would save her, that she was going to get out of this alive, and that I was going to have to spend the next five years apologizing for getting her involved in this mess.

Nothing wrong with thinking positive, Sam,

came Allison's words.

I nodded as we continued along. I led the way, periodically pausing and scouting ahead, occasionally pushing aside an errant tree branch or stepping over thicker bushes crowding the trail.

Soon, I found the red post in the ground, mostly hidden by thick creosote, huckleberry and something that could have been an overgrown fern. The path beyond was mostly nonexistent.

"Here?" asked Kingsley, his eyes shining like twin suns. God, we were such freaks, all of us.

"This is it," I said, and led the way. Behind me, despite his best efforts to stay quiet, he crashed through the forest like an oversized bear drunk on fermented blueberries.

The trail narrowed further, and I forced myself through the thickets and brambles, snagging my jeans and light jacket. I heard Allison behind me struggling a bit, and behind her, cursing under his voice, was Kingsley. We were a motley, ragtag bunch, an unlikely trio to take down a coven of vampires, or whatever they were called.

Covens are for witches, Sam, came Allison's words. *And Kingsley looks like he could take down a whole forest.*

Are you always in my head? I asked, finally spying the clump of boulders through the pines and spruces ahead.

These days, yes. We're very connected, Sam.

Lucky you, I thought, and sent her a mental wink.

And just like that, the tangle of branches and leaves and thorns and roots gave way to an open space, and a big pile of rocks.

"Here we are," I said. "The entrance."

40.

The opening was smaller than Kingsley had hoped.

"This could pose a problem," he said, which, of course, is exactly what I had said.

Kingsley, who'd scampered up onto the rocks with surprising agility, looking more like a hulking, hairy mountain goat than anything else, peered down into the dark hole that was surrounded by piles of boulders. That anyone consistently used this hole as an entry point to anything was beyond me. That my own flesh and blood sister had recently been forced down into this hole was unfathomable.

Poor Mary Lou.

Once again, I wished desperately that I could reach out to her in some way, but my sister and I were not in telepathic contact with each other, and neither were Danny or Fang; at least, in Fang's case, not anymore.

What have you done, Fang?

The opening was not obvious, even if a hiker had managed to work his way to this spot, which I suspected few had, and those who had might not live long enough to talk about it. Indeed, the boulders were surprisingly free of graffiti, which was a rarity anywhere in Los Angeles.

The three of us had climbed onto them and were presently looking down into a small opening. I could have been Alice looking down into the rabbit's hole. Except there were no rabbits down there, nor even a hallucinogenic Wonderland. No, nothing but murderous vampires.

And my sister. And Danny. And Fang.

Lord help us all.

Anyway, I could see through the darkness to a dirt floor below. I could also see imprints of shoes. Fresh imprints, too. Women's running shoes included. If I had to guess, those were Mary Lou's running shoes.

Seeing them now, and knowing she was close by, sent a fresh wave of panic through me.

I reported what I saw to the others, knowing that the entrance would lead down into a natural tunnel system.

"Tight squeeze," said Allison, "even for us girls."

She was right. How a grown man, no, a werewolf man, could expect to drop down into the hole, I didn't know.

"Yes, this is a very big problem," he said again.

"No," said Allison, "you are the big problem."

Believe it or not, I might have detected some flirtation in Allison's voice. Yes, she'd always had a crush on the big oaf. Anyway, Kingsley grunted at that, then reached down into the hole, grabbed hold of the edge of one of the flatter rocks, and did something that surprised even me. He pulled the sucker out. The huge rock—which was a borderline boulder—flipped out and tumbled down the pile, landing with a heavy thud in the dirt below.

We all looked down into the now-much-bigger hole.

"It's not a problem anymore," he said a little smugly.

Allison literally melted. "That was very impressive."

Kingsley looked at her, his eyes glowing wildly, blinked, and then shrugged. He might have just realized my best friend was smitten with him. "Yeah, well, I'm a bit of a monster."

"Well, it was just so...very impressive."

Cool your jets, I shot to her telepathically, and to Kingsley, I said, "It was also loud as hell...so much for the element of surprise."

"I thought we agreed that we *weren't* going to surprise anyone," said Kingsley, slightly annoyed at my reprimand.

"Well, not anymore," I said, and shot Lady Goo-Goo Eyes another hard stare, and then I leaped down into the tunnel entrance. "Come on," I said up to them, stepping aside, and soon my friends, one after the other, landed next to me.

41.

We were all in.

Although Kingsley and I could see just fine, Allison, despite her newfound witchy gifts and her ability to remote view, could not see in the dark. Which is why, presently, she was using the flashlight app on her Galaxy Note.

Kingsley, I couldn't help but notice, filled the narrow tunnel completely. In fact, he had to turn his massive shoulders slightly to stand reasonably comfortably. Even still, he hunched forward a little and looked, in general, miserable. Like a caged beast, perhaps.

The walls of the tunnels were mostly natural, but the ceiling, I saw, had clearly been carved out by someone. When this had been done, I wouldn't know, and, since none of us were archaeologists, we probably would never know. In fact, I wasn't even entirely sure vampires had hacked their way through this tunnel system. It could have been hobos or even a WWII bunker, for all I knew.

Of course, the only thing that mattered was who —or what—was using the caverns now.

And that would be vampires, and according to Allison, there were at least three of them.

Under the glow of Allison's cell phone app, I closed my eyes a final time and cast my thoughts out, down through the narrow tunnel, sweeping around a procession of ghosts—a host of lost spirits haunting the tunnels themselves...and into the caverns beyond, which were well within my range.

Once in the caverns, I noted the many torches flickering along the rock walls. No, vampires didn't need light, but light wasn't a bad thing, either. Perhaps these vamps wanted some additional light, perhaps the light was even for their human guests. I didn't know, and I didn't really care.

Next, I saw the first chamber. The room was decorated with a ragtag collection of furniture: old lounge chairs, garish couches and stools. Actually, the furniture looked like something from an old nightclub, which it very well might have been. How, exactly, the furniture had made it down here, I hadn't a clue, although I suspected there might be another entrance somewhere. I didn't know.

Anyway, on a purple camelback couch with an exaggerated hump sat a very old man who wasn't a man at all. He was a vampire, in fact, and I recognized him from Allison's own scan of the cavern. Of course, I recognized him from else-where, too. He was a vampire with a death wish. A vampire who, quite frankly, didn't want to be a vampire anymore, and had been willing to kidnap a boy—a boy he'd thought was my son—to force me to give him the ruby medallion, which would have reversed his vampirism, thus rendering him mortal. His plan hadn't worked, and now here he was, sitting casually on the couch, looking like an old creep at a nightclub, wearing black slacks and a white dress shirt, legs crossed. He appeared to be waiting for someone. Who that someone was, I could only guess.

I expanded my awareness out and into the next room, where I saw my ex-husband still secured to the desk. But this time, he wasn't alone. This time, Detective Hanner of the Fullerton Police Department was standing next to him, her hand on his head...and there was my sister, sitting in a straight-back chair, guarded by, of all people, Fang, who stood next to her.

Her arms were tied behind her back, her head was covered by a burlap sack. Her chest shuddered with each sob. Bile rose in my throat at her terror. *My sister!*

Hanner was holding a long blade away from her body, a blade that Danny kept his widened eyes on closely. My ex-husband, who had once been a loving and caring father, who had actually once even been a good husband before life—and the afterlife—had become too much for him, was scared shitless. I knew Danny and I knew that look. It was a look he'd given me many times after my turning.

Hanner's head was bowed slightly as she held the knife in one hand, the other still resting on Danny's head. And then, it occurred to me what she was doing.

She was scouting ahead, too. Or, rather, she was performing a sort of reverse surveillance. As Danny continued watching her, as blood dripped from his right hand, and as my sister continued weeping nearby, Hanner slowly raised her head and looked up...

And seemingly, directly at me.

She lifted her hand from Danny's head and waggled her finger at me slowly. She was admonishing me, and I suspected I knew why. If she could see me as I could see her, she had seen Kingsley and Allison with me, as well. I hadn't come alone, as I had been instructed.

And then she did the unthinkable.

She gave me a soulless smile—and plunged the knife deep into Danny's chest.

42.

I screamed and shot back into my body.

I was about to hurl myself down the hallway, as fast as I could, and into the caverns. In fact, it was only the hulking Kingsley in front of me who literally blocked my path that kept me from doing so.

"What happened?" Kingsley said, as I fought to get past him.

Allison answered for me, as all I could see was white-hot fury.

"Hanner stabbed Danny," I heard her say. "I saw it, too."

I was beyond thought or control. "I have to get to him. I have to get to him *now!*"

"We will, Sam."

"Kingsley, it's a trap," said Allison. "There are others waiting for her. I saw them. In particular, the old vampire."

"I'll take care of him," said Kingsley. "We do, after all, have some unfinished business." He was, of course, referring of their epic battle last year under the dome, when the old vampire had bested him and escaped. Kingsley looked grimly from me to Allison. "You remember the plan?" he asked her.

"I'll take care of the hunters," said my friend, who suddenly didn't seem very confident. She swallowed and I would have admired her bravery if I hadn't known the clock was ticking on my ex-husband.

This wasn't happening. I hadn't just seen my ex-husband get stabbed in the chest. I hadn't seen my sister with a bag over her head.

This wasn't happening, this wasn't happening.

No, no, no.

Kingsley gave me a final look, his handsome face full of determination and pity, and what happened next should have surprised me. Hell, it should have fascinated me. But it didn't.

Before our very eyes, Kingsley transformed.

Back in the minivan, he had told us he would do this. This had been, in fact, his plan. The old vampire was too strong for him in his human form. But the fight would be even in his changeling form. His werewolf form. I had spoken against this, reminding him that he lost all control of himself during transformation, and what Kingsley said next surprised and thrilled me at the time. "No, Sam. I lose control when the moon is full. Not so much when I *choose* to transform."

This had, of course, been news to me.

And now his transformation couldn't happen fast enough. Kingsley tore off his shirt and hunched forward, away from us. I had a sense that he didn't want us to see his face. He jerked and contorted and howled in what I assumed was agony. Allison slipped behind me, and I didn't blame her. The man she had a crush on was metamorphosing before our eyes.

The change took only seconds, perhaps twenty seconds in all. All the while, I thought of Danny with a knife in his chest.

Nothing you can do about it, if you're dead, I thought, which might have been my only rational thought during these moments. Yes, I knew we were walking into a trap. But they weren't expecting a full-fledged werewolf to make an appearance, a werewolf who would take on their oldest and strongest vampire.

Now Kingsley dropped to his knees and arched his back and what I saw there surprised even me. Hair had sprouted almost instantly. Short, silver-brown, thick hair.

No, *fur.*

Yes, I had seen what Kingsley turned into each full moon. A true wolfman, hulking, bipedal, frightening. What was emerging now was something different. It was, in fact, an actual wolf.

Within moments, a massive, four-legged wolf was now standing before us in the tunnel, looking haggard and pissed off, his mane hair erect, his tail held high in aggressive position. It turned once, looked back at us with Kingsley's same amber eyes, then it was off and running, faster than even I could run, which was pretty damn fast.

I was torn between running behind it and keeping Allison safe. Yes, I knew my friend had recently come into some powerful new skills—and could quite possibly take care of herself—but I couldn't take that chance. Ultimately, I held back with Allison, not wanting to leave my friend behind in the tunnels. The wolf that was Kingsley charged ahead and was soon out of sight.

43.

I paused just outside the cavern entrance.

While I waited for Allison to catch up, I listened to the horrific sounds echoing from within the big, underground room. I was tempted to dash into the cavern, but I didn't. That was what they wanted. I was sure of it. For me to act recklessly, danger-ously.

For me to die.

I held back, despite my natural instinct to rush forward and help. Kingsley had his hands full—or teeth full—in there. But he was a big boy. Or a big doggie. Instead, I closed my eyes and cast my thoughts forward a final time, into the cavern, and saw two people waiting not too far away. Whether they were vampires or not, I didn't know—but one thing was for certain.

Each was holding a crossbow notched with a

silver-tipped arrow.

Allison, breathing hard next to me, communicated with me silently: *I see them, Sam. Let me take care of them. Go get Danny and your sister.*

What do you mean?

Allison took point, stepping around me and into the cavern, holding her hands up before her.

***

She continued into the cavern in full witch mode, hands raised, palms out, like a battle was about to go down.

Her back was to me. I nearly ran to her, but waited, knowing what she was doing. She was clearing the way for me. I was expecting the worst. I was expecting a silver-tipped arrow to blossom in her chest.

But that didn't happen.

Instead, as the vicious fighting sounds of the werewolf and the vampire grew even louder and fiercer, Allison stood at the cavern entrance, unscathed, hands still up. Her hands, I saw, were shaking.

"Now, Sam!" she said, turning her head slightly toward me. Her arms were shaking even harder.

I was instantly in the cavern—and saw the two men guards now pinned against the rock walls, their crossbows crushed at their feet, their faces and hands physically forced into the stone wall behind them. They couldn't fight or struggle, or perhaps even breathe. They stood there, immobile, frozen, while Allison slowly walked forward, her hands still up and shaking even harder.

"Hurry, Sam!"

I was about to dash forward, into the adjoining cavern, when I saw a sight I wouldn't soon forget: Kingsley, in wolf form, was engaged in mortal combat with the vampire, the very old and very powerful vampire. As I watched, Kingsley went for the vampire's throat, hurling his long, muscular body through the air, only to absorb a devastating blow by the vampire that sent the wolf reeling, flipping head over tail, to crash into a nearby wall. The vampire, I saw, was covered with deep wounds, skin flapping at his scalp and neck. Yes, Kingsley had done some damage.

In the next room, I heard my sister scream.

I moved faster than I ever had in my entire existence.

44.

I knew Hanner was waiting for me.

In fact, she might have organized the others—the old vampire presently ensnared with Kingsley, and the two hunters waiting just inside the entrance —just to occupy my friends.

Yes, Hanner wanted me.

And only me.

Well, she was going to get me.

I doubted she would be waiting on the other side with a crossbow, nor would Fang. That didn't seem like her style. So, I took my chances and plunged through the opening, and into the second cavern.

***

Yes, there was my sister.

Fang stood next to her, too, holding a long

knife...a knife that was presently pressed against her fabric-covered throat, no doubt the reason why my sister had screamed in the first place.

Detective Rachel Hanner bent down next to my seated ex-husband, Danny, her ear pressed to his bloody lips, making a show of listening to him.

Hanner leaned in a little closer, and almost lovingly caressed the handle of the dagger that protruded from the center of his chest. I was too dumbfounded by the scene to act. I just stood there, absorbing the craziness, absorbing the fact that my life had so radically spun out of control that my jerk of an ex-husband was sitting with a dagger in his chest, and that my sister had a bag over her head, with another dagger pressed against her throat, held there by my one-time best friend, Fang.

I took another step into the room, and my sister screamed again, as Fang pressed the blade harder against her throat. I stopped. Hanner straightened and gave me a small smile, although her eyes did anything but smile.

"He keeps calling for you, Sam. I wonder why?" She moved around him as I saw Danny's body jerk a little. His eyelids fluttered. Blood bubbled up around the blade handle, which meant she had punctured a lung, but not his heart. At least, I didn't think she had. "Now, why would he be calling your name when he, in fact, called me?"

"Why would he call you?" I asked, and took another step into the room.

"Sam?" screamed Mary Lou, "Oh, my God,

Sam, what's happening?"

"It's going to be okay, Mary Lou," I said. "I'm going to get you out of here."

"It's very much *not* going to be okay, Samantha," said Hanner, now facing me. "Just ask your ex-husband. Oh, and there might have been a small chance that I came across your husband at his sleazy little strip club a few months ago, and told him to call me when his little vampire problem got out of hand."

Danny jerked his head; a small sound escaped from his bloody lips.

"There he goes again," said Hanner, shaking her pretty head, but not taking her eyes off me, eyes that burned with an inner flame. "Calling your name like you give a damn."

"I do give a damn," I said.

"And that's your problem, Samantha," said Hanner. "You give too much of a damn over these humans."

"You're not Hanner," I said, stepping forward again, and this time, Fang didn't press the knife any harder against my sister's throat. I noted that Fang looked nothing like the man I had once known. Fang and I had never had a physical relationship, and the truth was, we hadn't seen too much of each other outside of the bar where he'd worked, Hero's. Still, the man—or thing—in front of me, holding a knife to my sister's throat, looked dead and lost.

"No," said the female detective in front of me. She spoke in a slow, calculating, slightly lilting way, an accent I could not detect. "Hanner has taken, to use a modern idiom, a back seat. But rest assured, she's watching with interest from the shadows where she belongs. Where all of you belong."

"He needs help," I said. "Let him go. Let my sister go. You want me. I'm here."

"Oh, we want you all, Samantha Moon."

I looked at Fang, and decided to address him by his real name, "Aaron," I said. "What have you done? What have they done to you?"

"He can't talk, Sam," said Hanner.

I snapped my head around and looked at her. "Why the hell not?"

"He's been compelled not to, as you might have guessed. Just as he's being compelled to hold the knife to your sister. Just as he's being compelled to watch you die."

"Compelled by whom?" I asked, but knew the answer immediately. "Dominique."

"But of course, Samantha Moon. Only the most powerful vampires can compel another vampire. And Aaron here, or Eli, or Fang, as he still prefers to be called, has been such a good little boy. And quite the killer, too. Truly vicious. You should see him in action. He makes Mommy so very proud."

"You're sick."

"We're all sick, Sam."

"No," I said. "You're different. You're evil."

"We are mavericks, Samantha, nothing more, nothing less."

"What the hell does that mean?"

"It means we have seen how the world works, how the Universe works, and we have decided there is a better way."

"What way?"

"*Our* way, Samantha Moon. But to do that, you see, we need our sister to be free. You have bottled her up, so to speak, for far too long."

"You want to give her a new host."

"Yesss," Hanner hissed, although it was not Hanner who spoke to me. She looked over at my sister. "Yesss, and we found another, Sssamantha Moon. And she carries, of course, your bloodline."

"What about my bloodline?" I asked.

"You don't know, do you?"

"Know what?"

"Never mind that, Samantha. You'll be dead soon."

Hanner reached behind her back and pulled out an old-fashioned .38 revolver. "Not just any gun, Sam. This one happens to be equipped with silver bullets."

I almost sprang on her, believing wrongly that I could move faster than she could pull the trigger, except she was a fairly old vampire herself, and I would be dead before I took a step.

The fire in her eyes flared brightly.

I turned my shoulders as a shot rang out. Pain blasted my shoulder as the sound of the gunshot split the air. Mary Lou screamed. Even Danny made a noise. Most interesting was the noise I heard in the next chamber, the sound of something growling and the bellow of something dying.

But that all seemed very far away from me now.

"You are fast, Samantha Moon," said Hanner, approaching me, holding the gun out. "I've never known how you could anticipate another vampire. Then again, maybe it's something in your blood. Maybe it's something that's in your sister's blood, too. Something we can dig out, understand, and perhaps use."

I stumbled away from her, holding my shoulder, as her eyes flared again. The next shot shattered my elbow and I felt my right arm drop limp. I cried out for the first time in a long time. Mostly from the burning, the unending, goddamn burning.

She stepped around me, still holding the gun before her. She was smiling, but her eyes were dead...when I saw the slight change. The deadness was replaced with something close to compassion.

"I'm sorry, Sam," she said, the lilt in her voice gone. "I'm sorry it had to be this way. I liked you. I really did. I thought we could be friends. I thought we could be friends forever. But you wouldn't play by the rules. By *their* rules. Just know that I didn't want this for you."

She paused, and the deadness returned, replaced by the spark of fire just behind her pupils.

"Enough," said the accented voice.

She raised the gun, aimed it at my chest, and that was the last thing she ever did in this world.

The silver tip of Fang's knife blade appeared

through her chest.
    The bloodied silver tip.

45.

I was all alone with Danny.

"Allison has gone for help for you," I said. His head was on my lap as we sat together on the dirt and rock floor. My arm was messed up, but already healing. I kept it at my side. I could literally feel my bones moving, finding their way, forming and reforming.

"Who's Allison?" he asked. "Never mind."

I almost smiled. Indeed, a fat lot of good it did him to learn the name of one of my friends, especially if his condition didn't improve.

"I don't feel so good, Sam."

"I know you don't, you idiot."

With Fang's help, we had done our best to staunch Danny's bleeding.

Fang...he'd been released from his compulsion the instant that Kingsley had killed the old vampire. And when I'd said killed, I meant he could have been killed many dozens of times over. The old man was now nothing but chunks of bloody meat scattered around the cavern. Kingsley had stated that the old man had finally given up, and had just stood there when Kingsley had come for him. He was now certain the old man had wanted nothing more than to finally die. Kingsley had very much given him his wish.

And thus, he'd released Fang from his compulsion.

Instantly, Fang had sprung into action to save me.

Kingsley was now wearing my sweater around his waist, which now looked more like a loincloth. Truth was, with his scratched chest and thick shoulders and wild hair, he looked more like Conan the Barbarian than Orange County's most prominent defense attorney.

I shook my head at the absurdity of it all and returned my attention to my mortally wounded ex-husband.

"Why did you do it, you big idiot?" I asked.

Danny coughed and as he did so, more blood appeared around his bandage and from the corners of his mouth. "I hated you, Sam. You always seemed to get the better of me."

"I wasn't trying to get the better of you, you big friggin' moron."

"Do you mind not calling a dying man names, Sam?"

"You're not dying."

"You, better than anyone, could see that."

He was right, of course. I could see the aura around his body had darkened considerably in the last fifteen minutes, fifteen crazy minutes during which all of us were doing our best to make sense of what had just happened.

When Allison had finally released the two hunters, they'd dashed off, leaving behind their ruined crossbows and silver-tipped bolts. She was certain they had been compelled by Hanner. For as soon as she'd died, her control over them had vanished, as well. Yes, Hanner, my-one time drinking companion, was dead. The demon within her wasn't dead, of course. No, I had seen the black shadow pour from her dying mouth, to disappear into the ether, to one day find a new host.

Now Allison was off seeking help for Danny, and keeping in telepathic contact with me, too. At the moment, she had just made it to the parking lot, but she didn't have cell reception there either. I had given her my keys. She was just now getting into the minivan.

"I made so many mistakes, Sam," Danny said.

"I know."

He coughed. "Jesus, you didn't have to agree so fast."

"Well, you were a jerk and a moron and—"

"No name calling, remember? I know I screwed up."

"Royally," I said.

"I was afraid, Sam. Afraid of you. Afraid for my

life. I mean, I had no idea that such things existed."

"I'm not a *thing*, Danny. I was your wife. That was always your problem. You made me into a monster. I wasn't a monster, and you know it. I was fighting it and winning, and you abandoned me, abandoned us."

As I spoke, I couldn't help but notice his aura had darkened some more, and a deep, rich blackness was creeping through what had once had some color.

He coughed harder than before. He kept on coughing, and as he did so, the darkness kept spreading.

"Ah, Danny. I'm sorry this happened to you."

"I asked for it, Sam. And don't you dare save me. Don't you dare make me like you. Please."

"I won't, Danny."

He coughed harder than ever, and then lay back, wheezing. "I didn't know what I was doing, Sam. Hanner promised me she would help me get the kids back."

"You don't want the kids, Danny. They would only get in the way of your new...playboy lifestyle."

"That's where you're wrong, Sam. I love them more than you know."

His eyes closed and the darkness surrounded him completely.

"I know you love them, Danny," I said.

He didn't respond, of course.

My stupid idiot of an ex-husband had just died in my arms.

46.

It was weeks later.

I was in my office, working, doing anything I could to get my mind off Danny's death. We had left him in the cavern, along with the remains of the old vampire and Hanner. Kingsley had sealed the entrance with more rocks and destroyed another entrance we had found at the back of the caverns.

For all intents and purposes, the cavern had ceased to exist, and was now, in fact, a tomb, adding to its legions of dead three more lost souls.

There was no hiding Danny's death from my kids, especially when I had a mind-reading daughter. So, I had told them what had happened. I told them that their dad had died trying to be with them, that their dad had made friends with the wrong people, and that their dad had died telling me how much he loved them, his last words, in fact.

It had been a hell of a shitty week.

Yes, I had asked my kids to keep one more whopping big secret. I asked them not to let the world know that their dad had died. Yes, I was a horrible mother, but the world at large needed to think that Danny had disappeared, perhaps with a stripper prospect, or perhaps because of some dirty business dealings. These explanations weren't far from the truth. Hanner and Fang had disappeared months earlier, back when Fang had first turned. Hell, Fang didn't technically exist, anyway, having been on the run since his escape from the insane asylum two decades earlier.

I had all of this on my mind in the weeks that followed, weeks during which I threw myself into my work, and threw myself into anything to avoid thinking about my lying, cheating ex-husband, my ex-husband who I suddenly missed with all my heart, my ex-husband who I forgave and would forever forgive.

Sanchez had also come by with questions of his own. I told him what I knew. I even told him about the caverns under the Los Angeles River. I told him that he had been compelled to act as a sort of puppet for Hanner.

I told him all of this, then took his hand and looked him deeply in the eyes, and then compelled him to forget it all. I told him to go home to his psycho wife and to forget anything about vampires. I told him to close his related cases and to write all three off as animal attacks. I told him I thought he was very handsome, but asked him to forget that I'd said that, too.

It was with these heavy thoughts, as I was leaning down and filing papers away in my office, when I heard a whisper of clothing and the swish of pant legs.

I looked up to find Fang standing in my doorway.

47.

"I'm sorry about your ex-husband," he said.

The truth was, I had been pissed at Fang, too. His desire to be a vampire—his own personal compulsion—had led to circumstances and events that had led, in turn, to Danny's murder.

But I knew that wasn't fair, either. Fang had just wanted to be a vampire, to be immortal, to live the life of characters in books and movies, but he had not fully comprehended the horror of the reality of such an existence.

The reality was, of course, that something very dark and sinister now called Fang's body home.

"Thank you," I said. "Danny was a good man who made bad choices."

Fang was seated in one of my three client chairs. Yes, I was ever the optimist. His long legs were crossed, and the drape of his jeans hung neatly. He was wearing leather boots that looked expensive. I suspected that Hanner had dressed and splurged on him these past few months. He was, after all, supposed to be her golden boy. As in, the perfect vampire and perfect killer. I didn't want to know what Fang had done, or how many he had killed these past few months.

I could see the fire just behind his pupils, the fire that hadn't been there when I'd first met him for drinks last year, back when he had finally revealed his super-secret identity, and I'd realized the extent to which I had been stalked. Back then, he had been a bit star-struck, awed to be in the presence of a real vampire. He had been excited and goofy and funny and charming.

Now, he was none of that.

Now, he was controlled, reserved, cautious and careful. He watched me closely, rarely taking his brooding eyes off of me. His mannerisms were nonexistent; instead, he kept his hands folded on one knee, hands that had once poured us drinks at Hero's, where I had first met him, back when Mary Lou and I had thought he was just another cute bartender, back when my marriage had been shaky, at best. Now, those hands had been compelled to hold a silver blade to my sister's neck.

"You miss him," said Fang.

"Danny was my first love. He was the father of my children. He died in my arms." I looked away. "And he was never given a proper funeral. Yes, I miss the big idiot."

Fang looked down for the first time. He adjusted the drape of his jeans then returned his hands to his knee. "I'm sorry that I played a part in his death, Sam."

I nodded and wiped my eyes and looked back at him. It was, of course, hard to tell how sorry he was, with no inflection or emotion in his voice.

"I miss you, Sam," he said. "I know now may not be the time to say it, and, for all I know, you're still dating that muscle-bound boxer or even Kingsley or someone else, but I want you to know that I miss you every day. I missed you even when I was compelled to do bad things. I missed you while I silently screamed inside my head. I miss you every day, every hour, every minute. I never stop thinking about you."

"Did you kill, Fang?"

"Yes. Many."

"Were you compelled to kill?"

"Sometimes."

"And, what about the other times?"

He looked away. "No."

I bit my lip and fought the tears that threatened to come. "I think you should leave."

He nodded once and stood smoothly on long legs. He crossed the room and paused at my office door.

"I'm sorry I failed you, Sam."

He looked at me for a long moment and something hit me, something deep in my heart. I suddenly remembered the love I felt for him, the deep longing to have him back in my life.

As he turned to leave, I said, "Wait, Fang."

He looked back. "Yes, Moon Dance?"

I hadn't heard him say my old username in so long that I nearly lost it right there. Instead, I kept it together and said, "I miss you, too."

He smiled and I saw the tears in his eyes.

"More than you know."

The End

About the Author:

J.R. Rain is an ex-private investigator who now writes full-time. He lives in a small house on a small island with his small dog, Sadie. Please visit him at www.jrrain.com.

Made in the USA
Monee, IL
29 July 2022